# Mary Anne and Miss Priss

**Other books by
Ann M. Martin**

*Rachel Parker, Kindergarten Show-off*
*Eleven Kids, One Summer*
*Ma and Pa Dracula*
*Yours Turly, Shirley*
*Ten Kids, No Pets*
*Slam Book*
*Just a Summer Romance*
*Missing Since Monday*
*With You and Without You*
*Me and Katie (the Pest)*
*Stage Fright*
*Inside Out*
*Bummer Summer*

BABY-SITTERS LITTLE SISTER series
THE BABY-SITTERS CLUB mysteries
THE BABY-SITTERS CLUB series
(see back of book for a more complete listing)

# Mary Anne and Miss Priss
## Ann M. Martin

AN
**APPLE**
PAPERBACK

SCHOLASTIC INC.
New York Toronto London Auckland Sydney

Cover art by Hodges Soileau

No part of this publication may be reproduced in whole or in part, or stored in a retrieval system, or transmitted in any form or by any means, electronic, mechanical, photocopying, recording, or otherwise, without written permission of the publisher. For information regarding permission, write to Scholastic Inc., 555 Broadway, New York, NY 10012.

ISBN 0-590-47011-6

12 11 10 9 8 7 6 5 4 3 2 1        4 5 6 7 8/9

Printed in the U.S.A.        40

First Scholastic printing, March 1994

*The author gratefully acknowledges*
*Jahnna Beecham*
*and*
*Malcolm Hillgartner*
*for their help in*
*preparing this manuscript.*

# CHAPTER 1

"I see another one!" Margo Pike cried happily. "That makes four robins today."

It was Wednesday afternoon and I was baby-sitting at the Pike house. After what seemed like an endless winter, we were looking for signs of spring. Nicky Pike, who's nine, had spotted some daffodils poking up by the backyard fence. And five-year-old Claire Pike was positive she had seen a "flutterby." (That's what she calls butterflies.)

"It was orange and black and buzzed all around our house," Claire said solemnly. "The triplets don't believe me, but I really saw it."

"I believe you," I said, ruffling her chestnut brown hair. All of the Pike kids have that same shade of hair, although Mallory's is more reddish. And all eight (yes, eight!) have blue eyes. Mallory Pike, who is eleven and the oldest, is the only one with curly hair.

Mallory and I were baby-sitting together because her seven brothers and sisters were home, and it takes more than one person to watch that many children. Mallory's mom had to attend a library trustee meeting that afternoon, and Mallory's father wouldn't be home from work until five-thirty. So Mrs. Pike had called the Baby-sitters Club to find someone to help Mallory baby-sit. The Baby-sitters Club, or BSC for short, is one of the most important things in my life. You see, I'm the secretary and one of the original members. But I'm getting ahead of myself. First I should tell you who I am. Then I'll tell you about the club.

My name's Mary Anne Spier. I'm thirteen and in the eighth grade at Stoneybrook Middle School. I have brown eyes, short dark hair, and I'm pretty short myself. Most people say I am very sensitive, and I guess they're right. Usually, I don't mind being sensitive. I think it makes me understanding of other people. My friends know that when they have problems, I'll listen and be sympathetic. The bad part is, I cry at the least little thing. (I still get weepy over *Pollyanna*, and I bet I've seen that movie at least twenty times)

My mother died when I was really little, so my father had to raise me by himself. He had an awful lot of rules for me. For example, I had to wear little girl jumpers and dresses,

2

and keep my hair in braids (to make the six-year-old look complete). I know he meant well, but it was terribly frustrating.

Luckily, that has changed, partly because I convinced him I was growing up, and partly because he got married again (more about that later). Now I can dress however I like — within reason. And I can wear clip-on earrings, which I think look pretty good.

Dad and I used to live on Bradford Court, next door to Kristy Thomas, my first best friend. It was Kristy's idea to form the Baby-sitters Club. Besides being a great idea, it was also a big help to me. I'm not only sensitive, I'm shy, which makes it kind of difficult to meet new people. Thanks to the BSC, I made seven more close friends, including one boyfriend, Logan Bruno.

What can I say about Logan? He's smart and funny, is incredibly cute, and has this charming Southern accent. (That's because he's from Kentucky.) When Logan first moved to Stoneybrook, a lot of girls at SMS thought he was cute, but he picked me to be his girlfriend. That was one of the biggest surprises of my life. How did it happen? Over baby-sitting, of course. First, Logan volunteered to join the BSC. Then we baby-sat for the Rodowskys together. After that Logan asked me to go to the Remember September dance. Then one thing

3

led to another and pretty soon we were going steady. We've gone through some rough spots, and we even broke up once, because Logan was getting a little too possessive. But he agreed to give me more space, and lately our relationship has been great.

Would you believe me if I told you that I not only met my boyfriend through the BSC, but my sister, too? Well, it's true. Growing up with just my dad, I always dreamed of having a sister. Of course, I knew it could never happen. Then I met Dawn Schafer, who had just moved to Connecticut with her mom and her younger brother, Jeff. Dawn joined the BSC and became my other best friend. We didn't know it when we met, but her mom and my father had been high school sweethearts. We found that out while looking through some old high school yearbooks that belonged to Dawn's mom, and we decided it would be fun for our parents to meet up again, so we arranged it. And guess what? They fell in love all over again. Before long they were married, and my dream had come true. I had a sister. (Dawn is really my stepsister, of course, but she feels like a genuine sister.)

After the wedding, Dad and I left Bradford Court and moved in with Dawn and Sharon. (Dawn's brother, Jeff, had decided he was much happier living with his dad in Califor-

4

nia.) Now we all live in an old farmhouse that was built in the seventeen-hundreds. It even has a secret passage which we think may be haunted!

Things were a little bumpy at first, because we have such different habits. My dad is Mister Organization. He categorizes everything — including his clothes — and he likes to keep things neat as a pin. Sharon is the opposite. She's really absentminded and does the craziest things, such as leaving her high-heels in the vegetable drawer of the refrigerator, or putting the pruning shears in the bathroom cabinet. Another big difference between our two families is that Sharon and Dawn (and Jeff) are practically vegetarians. They don't eat red meat, and they actually like tofu burgers and brown rice, whereas Dad and I prefer normal food, such as steak and french fries.

Still, despite our differences, we were getting along fine until last fall, when Dawn decided that she really missed her father and brother. After a good deal of soul-searching she asked Sharon and her dad if she could spend some time in California. It was a difficult decision for both parents, but in the end they agreed that Dawn could go. I think I understand why Dawn wanted to leave, but that doesn't stop me from missing her like crazy.

And she's not the only fellow baby-sitter I

miss. The club lost Mallory (sort of) over the winter, too. Just after Halloween, Mal came down with mononucleosis. Mono is a disease that affects your glands and makes you tired all the time. For about a month, Mallory had to stay home from school and not do anything. She spent the days in bed or on the couch. Finally she was able to attend school, but she had to go straight home afterward to rest — she still couldn't participate in any after-school activities. Mal hated missing so much school, and was bored to distraction, but the worst part of mono, for her, was when her parents made her drop out of the Baby-sitters Club. (They do still allow her to sit for her own family, though.) It was kind of hard on the rest of us. Everybody in the club had to take extra sitting jobs to make up for the loss.

Between the winter weather, Dawn's departure, and Mal's mono, I'd had plenty of reasons to feel blue. Then, on top of everything else, Logan's volleyball team made it to the state tournament, which was nice, in a way, but it meant I hardly saw him at all. To battle my blahs, I recently volunteered to help Mrs. Kishi with a fund-raising Readathon at the library. That turned out to be an adventure in itself. (Would you believe that I, shy Mary Anne, helped to catch an arsonist who was setting fires with books?) I was sorry when the

Readathon ended, and I kind of miss my job at the library, but the good news is — winter has ended, volleyball season is over, and Logan is calling me again.

"I'm so glad spring is coming," Mallory said, taking a big breath of fresh air and lying back in the moist green grass of her backyard. "I finally feel well."

"Maybe your parents will let you rejoin the BSC now," I said, nibbling on a blade of grass. "You've been baby-sitting quite a lot lately, haven't you?"

Mallory frowned. "I can only sit for my brothers and sisters, which doesn't make sense." Mallory raised up on one elbow. "I mean, I'm spending so much time baby-sitting for them, I might as well be baby-sitting for other kids. What does it matter where I sit?"

"Maybe your parents are worried that you might get sick again, and they're just being cautious."

"Too cautious, if you ask me," Mallory griped. "I really do feel well, but my parents won't believe me. It's so frustrating."

Before I could say anything to comfort Mallory, the triplets appeared, sporting identical scowls. Byron and Jordan stood on either side of Adam, looking like guards with their arms folded across their chests. Adam spoke first.

"We've decided that this is the last time we

will have a baby-sitter," Adam said firmly. "We're ten years old. That's too old to be baby-sat." He winced when he said "baby-sat," as if just pronouncing the word hurt.

"Have you talked to your mom and dad about this?" I asked.

"Yes!" Adam replied. "But they won't listen."

"It's just not fair," Jordan chimed in. "Baby-sitting is for babies. We're in the fifth grade. We're practically grown-up!"

"Yeah," Byron added. "I mean, we know long division and how to use a microscope."

I wasn't sure what that had to do with being grown-up but I didn't say a word. I couldn't. The boys were talking too fast for me to get a word in.

"I make my bed." Adam ticked off his accomplishments on one hand. "I clean up my room and do my chores. *And* I stay up till ten o'clock on weeknights."

"I ride my bike after dark," Byron added. "That's got to mean something."

"Besides," Jordan burst out, "Mallory is only a year older than us. Why should she get to be on her own and not us?"

At this point Mallory sat up and shouted over her brothers, "Look, I'm not getting any special privileges! Mom and Dad may let me baby-sit, but right now only with you guys. I

8

feel like a prisoner in my own house."

"So do we!" the boys yelled back.

So much for daffodils and robins. The feeling in the air now was more like a winter blizzard than a warm spring breeze. But instead of running for shelter, I tried to help. "I think you all have reasonable complaints," I began. "But I'm not sure what to do about them."

"Me either." Mallory sighed.

Before we could work anything out, Mrs. Pike returned. "How did everything go?" she asked as she searched through her purse.

"We had a wonderful time finding signs of spring," I replied. "Claire found a flutterby, Nicky discovered some daffodils, and Margo counted four robins." I didn't mention the triplets' decision. I figured they could bring that up themselves.

"Can you stay for some lemonade?" Mrs. Pike asked.

I checked my watch. Five-fifteen. "Thank you. I'd love to, but today is Wednesday and we have a BSC meeting at five-thirty."

"Oh, that's right." Mrs. Pike nodded. "I forgot."

"I didn't forget," Mallory said, stepping forward.

Mal and I looked at Mrs. Pike. I think we were half hoping she would tell Mallory to go ahead and join me, but no such luck.

"Tell everyone hi for me," Mal said as I moved to the door. Then she added pointedly, "Tell them I *really* miss them."

"Okay," I said. "I know they miss you, too."

I hurried down the front steps and across the lawn. Just before I turned the corner, I glanced over my shoulder and saw Mallory waving sadly from her front porch. I felt terrible for her, but I wasn't sure what I could do. She certainly seemed fine to me. Maybe, like the triplets, she needed to take her complaint to her parents.

# CHAPTER 2

When I arrived at Claudia Kishi's, Kristy was just crossing the street. She was carrying her Kid-Kit, because she had been baby-sitting for the Perkins kids.

"We have exactly one minute to get upstairs and find a seat before the meeting starts," Kristy said formally. Then she broke into a big grin and shouted, "Race you!"

Kristy is president of the Baby-sitters Club. Mostly because it was her idea, but also because she is a real leader. (Some people might even call her bossy.) She also coaches a softball team called Kristy's Krushers. Kristy doesn't care much about fashion. She usually wears blue jeans, a turtleneck or a T-shirt, and running shoes. We call it her uniform. Sometimes she wears a baseball cap with a picture of a collie on it, in memory of her family's wonderful old collie, Louie.

When Louie was a puppy, Kristy lived next

door to me on Bradford Court, with her mom (who was divorced) and three brothers — David Michael, who is seven now, and Sam and Charlie, who are in high school. But then her mom met Watson Brewer, a really nice guy who also happens to be an actual millionaire. Watson has two children from his first marriage: seven-year-old Karen and four-year-old Andrew. Anyway, Watson asked Kristy's mom to marry him, she said yes, and the Thomases moved across town to Watson's mansion. Soon, Watson and Kristy's mom adopted a little girl from Vietnam, whom they named Emily Michelle, and then Kristy's grandmother, Nannie, moved in to help run the house and take care of Emily (who's two and a half). It's a good thing the house is so big, because when Karen and Andrew visit (which is every other weekend) ten people live there.

Our vice-president is Claudia Kishi. We hold our meetings at her house in her room, because she has a phone with her very own personal number. Can you believe it? Claudia is one of the coolest people I know. She's also totally gorgeous. She's Japanese-American and has long shiny black hair and a perfect, creamy complexion (which is amazing considering all the junk food she eats). Claud is a fabulous artist and can do just about anything

— paint, sculpt, design jewelry, you name it. Her artistic flair shows up in everything she wears and does. For example, Claud rarely buys Christmas and Valentine's Day cards. She makes her own. Sometimes they're really sharp collages, with different colored tissue paper and pictures from magazines, and sometimes they're pen-and-ink drawings, but they are always unique. I've kept every one she's given me.

Claudia is smart, but she's not a very good student. That might not matter so much, except that her older sister, Janine, is a true genius. Janine is so smart that she's taking college courses while she's in high school! Still, even though English and spelling are Claud's least favorite subjects, she has become a staff writer for the *SMS Express*, our school newspaper. Isn't that neat? She started a column called Claudia's Personals when she was looking for the perfect boy, and it was such a hit that she's kept it going. Claud still hasn't found the perfect guy, but she hasn't given up hoping.

Stacey McGill is our club treasurer, mostly because she's really good at math. Stacey and Claudia are best friends, which makes sense because they both love math so much. Not! They're really cool dressers, but Stacey's a little more trendy. In fact, Stacey is the most sophisticated of all of us, probably because she grew up in New York City, and she still goes there quite often to visit her father, who is divorced from her mom. That's probably why she always knows the newest styles and is the first to wear them. Her hair is long, blonde, and permed and always looks as though some famous hairdresser just styled it. It sounds like Stacey has it all, right? Unfortunately, she has one thing she doesn't want — diabetes. That's a disease which prevents her body from manufacturing enough of this chemical called insulin, which helps you process sugar. Stacey has to give herself injections of insulin every single day. (Can you imagine? I'd probably faint.) She also has to monitor everything she eats. Too much sugar, or too little, and she could get really sick. She never makes a fuss about it, though. I admire her for that.

One more thing about Stacey. She's in love! Her boyfriend is this great-looking boy (as cute as Logan, but not really my type) named Robert. He used to be a star basketball player, but recently he quit the team. Why? In part, to protest Stacey's not getting chosen for the cheerleading squad. She was clearly the best candidate, and everyone knew it, but that was the problem. The other girls thought she was too good. (Ick. Talk about not my type. . . .) Robert also had a real problem with our

14

school's sports obsession, so even when the cheerleaders finally reconsidered, and offered Stacey a place on the squad (which she turned down), he refused to rejoin the basketball team. I think Stacey and Robert are both a lot happier because of their decisions. The rough time they went through has brought them closer together.

Getting back to our club roster, this is where I fit in. I'm the BSC secretary, because I have the neatest handwriting and I am really organized (kind of like my dad). I've already told you a lot about myself, so I'll move on to alternate officer. Dawn Schafer is usually our alternate officer but, as I mentioned, she's away in California. She baby-sits out there, too, with a group of friends who call themselves the We ♥ Kids Club. (Yes, Kristy's great idea went bi-coastal!) Dawn's west coast life isn't all sun and surfers, though. When she arrived in California, she discovered that her father's relationship with his girlfriend, Carol, was much more serious than she had thought. Dawn's never been too fond of Carol, and when her dad announced that they were going to get married, Dawn ran away. Here's the really bad part: she used her father's credit card to buy a plane ticket, without asking, and flew back here to Connecticut. Naturally, this didn't go over too well. Dawn's mom was so angry that she booked Dawn on the next flight back to California, and didn't even let her see any members of the BSC before she left. (Except me, of course — and our reunion wasn't exactly festive. It was hard to enjoy catching up with Dawn when words like "deceitful" and "irresponsible" were echoing through our house.) Sharon and Dawn's dad also insisted that she pay them both back for the plane tickets. Flights across the country aren't cheap, so now Dawn is working like crazy to pay her parents back. To make matters worse, Dawn's behavior provoked a big fight between her dad and Carol, and they broke off their engagement. Now Dawn feels incredibly guilty, even though her dad assured her that the breakup wasn't her fault. I wish I could be there for her. Better yet, I wish she'd hurry back!

Shannon Kilbourne, who, like Logan, has been an associate BSC member, is taking Dawn's place for the time being. (As associates, Logan and Shannon don't regularly come to meetings, and they take sitting jobs when none of us are available.) Shannon lives in Kristy's new neighborhood, and goes to Stoneybrook Day School, across town. When they first met, Kristy thought Shannon was a snob, but that was just a misunderstanding. They're friends now. In fact, when Louie, Kristy's collie, died, Shannon gave the Thomases one of her own dog's puppies. David Michael named the puppy Shannon, which I thought was awfully sweet, but it does get confusing when Shannon the dog and Shannon the person are both over at Kristy's house.

Shannon has a ski jump nose, super high cheekbones, and these great big blue eyes. She's a serious student, which is one reason she had never wanted to be a full BSC member. Her homework and school clubs have always come first. Luckily for us, she's managed to clear her schedule enough to fill in for Dawn.

That's everybody except the junior officers — Mallory Pike (whom I'd just finished sitting with) and Jessica Ramsey. Mal and Jessi are best friends, partly because they have a lot in common and partly because they are so different. Here's what they have in common: they're eleven, in the sixth grade, and have pierced ears (they had them pierced at the same time). Both are horse crazy and spend a lot of time reading books about horses, especially those written by Marguerite Henry. Both are the oldest kids in their families.

What's different? Jessi is black, with long, long legs and big brown eyes, and Mal is white, with curly red-brown hair, glasses, and braces (which make her feel like an ugly duckling these days). There are eight kids in Mal's family, while Jessi is one of three. She has a sister, Becca, who is eight-and-a-half, and a baby brother, Squirt (his real name is John Philip). Jessi is a talented ballerina and hopes to dance with a famous ballet company some day; Mallory dreams of being a famous writer and illustrator of children's books.

The Baby-sitters Club meets every Monday, Wednesday, and Friday from five-thirty to six. That's when clients call to schedule baby-sitting jobs. That was the essence of Kristy's brilliant idea: to give parents one number at which they could reach many experienced sitters. I'm in charge of the record book, which means I have to keep track of everyone's activities, and determine who is available to baby-sit. I know this sounds amazing, but I have never made a scheduling mistake (knock on wood). Stacey collects the dues, helps to pay Claud's phone bills, and gives Kristy's brother money for driving her to the meetings. Stacey also gives the rest of us cash when we need to buy new items for our Kid-Kits.

Kid-Kits, another one of Kristy's great ideas, are cardboard cartons filled with art supplies, and our old toys and games. Each of us decorated our box (with artistic advice from Claudia), and on rainy days, or sometimes just for fun, we take them with us to our sitting jobs.

18

The kids love them, and they are great ice-breakers.

During each meeting we schedule jobs, talk about new projects to do with the kids, and write in the BSC notebook. Unlike the record book, the notebook is a kind of journal in which we record what's going on with our clients. If a kid is having trouble in school, or her parents are divorcing, or he's convinced a monster lives under his bed, it helps to know ahead of time.

So, that's the Baby-sitters Club and how it works. Now, back to my race with Kristy. She took the stairs four at a time and crossed the doorsill into Claud's room one second before I did. She landed in her director's chair just as Claud's digital clock turned from five-twenty-nine to five-thirty.

"I win!" Kristy said, raising one fist in victory.

"Not fair," I huffed, flopping onto Claud's bed. "You got a head start."

Logan, who was attending the meetings this week, grinned at me. "When are you going to learn never to get into a race with Kristy? She can beat practically anybody in the eighth grade. Guys included."

Kristy blushed with pride and grinned. "Thanks, Logan. And on that note, I officially call this meeting to order. Any new business or announcements?"

"I have some good news." Claud held up a plastic bag. "I finally found this bag of potato chips that I hid in the back of my closet two months ago. Anybody want one?"

Stacey, who was stretched out on the bed on her stomach, wrinkled her nose. "Ew! Gross! Two-month-old chips? They'll be stale."

Claudia pulled the bag open and took a loud, crunchy bite of a chip. "Nope. They were vacuum sealed. Mmmmmm!"

Shannon was sitting on the floor at the foot of the bed, next to Jessi. She waved her hand excitedly to get everyone's attention. "I have some really big news. Astrid's going to have puppies again!"

"You're kidding!" Kristy yelped.

Astrid is Shannon's Bernese mountain dog, and the mother of Kristy's dog, which is why Kristy was so excited. In case you're wondering, Bernese mountain dogs look sort of like St. Bernards except they're black and white instead of brown and white.

"Ooooh, I wish I could have one of the puppies," Kristy said. "Wouldn't that be neat? Two Bernies."

Stacey nodded. "I bet they'll be darling. Tiny balls of fur."

Shannon giggled. "They don't stay tiny for long. Before you know it they turn into big, teddy bears, and then *huge* loveable dogs."

"That shed and slobber all over you," Logan added with a grin.

"They do not slobber!" Kristy said indignantly.

"They do too!" Logan teased. "I've seen your dog walk around with big, long strings of drool that almost touch the ground."

"Ew! Gross!" Claudia said.

Luckily for everyone, the phone rang before Logan could give us any more details about Shannon (the dog's) slobber.

"Baby-sitters Club, this is Stacey. . . . Oh, hi, Mrs. Prezzioso."

We waited patiently as Stacey wrote down the details of Mrs. Prezzioso's call. When she hung up, Stacey was frowning.

"Mrs. Prezzioso needs a sitter for Jenny every weekday afternoon, indefinitely."

"*Every* weekday?" I gasped.

Stacey nodded, repeating, "Indefinitely."

The others sat in silence while I checked the schedule book. I shook my head. "It's hard to schedule a job like this. I think everyone in the BSC is busy at least one day a week."

"And even if we're not," Stacey said, "I don't think any of us wants to give up every single afternoon."

21

Kristy bit her lip. "No one has ever asked us to make this kind of commitment. It's like taking on a permanent job."

I stared at the schedule book. "Jessi's out, she has dance class three times a week," I mumbled. "Kristy has Krushers practice and Claud needs time for the newspaper, plus she has art class. Stacey and Logan are busy this week and Shannon has a French club dinner." I looked up at the group. "I'm the only one who could possibly do it — this week — but I don't think I'm up for working five days. I could maybe do three days each week, though."

Then Kristy suggested, "Why don't you pick three regular days, and we'll fill in the remaining ones on a job-by-job basis?"

I agreed to try it for a few weeks. I chose Mondays, Wednesdays, and Thursdays. The last half of our meeting was really crazy. I tried to schedule everyone into the Tuesday and Friday slots. No one else was available for the first Tuesday so I decided to take that day, too. It was nearly six o'clock when I called Mrs. Prezzioso back to tell her the news. She was thrilled and couldn't stop thanking me.

"You girls are wonderful," she said. (Oh, well. I knew she meant Logan, too.) "Simply wonderful. You've saved my life."

I didn't think to ask Mrs. Prezzioso why she needed a sitter for every afternoon of the week, or why it was just for Jenny and not Andrea, the baby. I guess I figured I'd find out on Monday.

# CHAPTER 3

$D$*ing dong.*

As I waited for someone to answer the Prezziosos' doorbell Monday afternoon, I thought about the first time I'd baby-sat for Jenny. She'd acted so prim and proper and had been so fussy about the food she ate and the clothes she wore, that we'd often call her Miss Priss. She was three then, and an only child. Now Jenny's four and has a baby sister, and she's much more relaxed about her clothes. She even wears (gasp) pants sometimes.

I heard the sound of tiny feet running to answer the door. Then a high voice asked, "Who is it, please?"

Jenny's mother has taught her never to open the door until she knows who is outside. I think that's good advice.

"Hi, Jenny," I called. "It's me, Mary Anne."

There was a short silence. Then Jenny said, "Mary Anne Spier?"

I smiled to myself. How many Mary Annes could she know? "Yes," I replied. "It's Mary Anne Spier. Your baby-sitter."

I heard the lock turning. When the front door opened, I took one look at Jenny and nearly fainted. She was covered from head to toe in lace.

Two pink lace bows perched in her dark brown hair. Her pink dress had a delicate lace collar, lacey puffed sleeves, and a big satin-and-lace sash around the waist. Even her socks were topped with lace. Jenny looked more like a doll — the kind you collect, not play with — than a real little girl. Miss Priss was back.

I stammered, "J-Jenny, what's the occasion? Are you going to a party or something?"

Jenny blinked her blue eyes at me. "No. This is how I always dress."

Hmmmmm. Something wasn't right. But before I could quiz Jenny any more about her appearance, Mrs. Prezzioso appeared at the top of the stairs. In her arms was baby Andrea, who looked like a miniature version of Jenny, although she didn't have enough hair for bows. She wore a lace-covered bonnet instead.

"You two look gorgeous," I said. "Like something out of a magazine."

"Thank you, dear," Mrs. Prezzioso replied as she swept down the stairs. "Sorry I can't chat, but Andrea and I are in a very big hurry.

25

I've left the number where you can reach me on the refrigerator." Mrs. Prezzioso continued to give me instructions as she gathered her coat and opened the front door. "Take care, my angel," she called, blowing Jenny a kiss. "Mommy will be back soon."

Jenny stood in the entryway and stared at the closed front door. Her chin quivered and for just a second, I thought she might cry.

"Would you like to see what I've brought in my Kid-Kit?" I asked, hoping to distract her.

"No, thank you," Jenny said, quickly recovering. "I would like a drink of juice, please. I'm very thirsty."

Jenny and I headed for the kitchen and as we passed the gilded hall mirror, she paused to study her reflection. I watched her check the front and back view of her dress to make sure everything was in perfect order. Then she carefully smoothed a strand of hair back into place. Yes, she was definitely acting like the old Miss Priss.

I poured Jenny a glass of apple juice while she sat primly at the dining room table. Unfortunately, when she took her first sip of juice, a drop of it fell onto her dress.

"Oh, no!" She stared in horror at the little spot.

"Here, Jenny." I grabbed a towel from the

kitchen and handed it to her. "We'll just blot the juice with this. You'll never know it was there."

Jenny leapt to her feet. "I can't wear this dress. It's ruined."

Before I could stop her, Jenny raced up the stairs. By the time I caught up with her, she'd removed all her clothes — socks, hair bows, and all. Too surprised to say anything, I watched as she changed into a pale blue dress with matching socks and ribbons.

"You look very pretty," I said as she finished tying the ribbons. "But I really don't think you needed to change all of your clothes."

"Mommy likes for us to stay clean," was Jenny's reply. Then she did a very strange thing. She went into the bathroom and washed her hands, which didn't look at all dirty to me. She scrubbed and scrubbed, being careful not to splash any water on herself. "There," she murmured, when she'd dried her hands thoroughly. "Much better."

Downstairs, Jenny refused to drink any more juice, for fear that she might spill again. Instead she went into the living room and sat on a straight-backed chair with her hands folded in her lap.

I stood in the doorway, waiting to see what

would happen next. She just sat. "Jenny?" I finally said. "I thought we might play outside. Would you like that?"

Jenny glanced out the picture window in the living room. The sun was shining brightly and it did look enticing. "Well, maybe. Just for a little while."

"Why don't you change into your play clothes?" I had visions of a speck of something dirtying Jenny's dress, followed by another frantic race for the closet. "That way we could go to the park."

"No. I don't want play clothes," Jenny said, folding her arms firmly across her chest. "They make me look ugly."

"That's not true. You have some very nice pants."

She does, too. Unlike most kids, whose play clothes consist of old jeans and faded tees, Jenny wears outfits that match, and look brand new.

Jenny shook her head. "I'm not going to change, so I may as well stay inside."

I looked longingly at the bright day outside and made a decision. "We could both use some sunshine," I declared. "Come on. Let's go for a walk."

Before Jenny would step outside, she insisted on checking her appearance in the hall mirror again. "My hair looks messy," she complained. "I think I should comb it first."

That was it. I grabbed her by the hand and practically dragged her through the front door. "Forget your hair. If it gets messed up on our walk you can fix it when we come back."

It was a perfect time to be outside. The trees were budding and the sun felt wonderfully warm on my face.

*Beep! Beep!* a horn blew behind us on the sidewalk. It was Matthew Braddock riding his bike. Matt is deaf and communicates with Ameslan (that's American Sign Language). Today he was leading Buddy Barrett and Nicky Pike in a bicycle parade down the sidewalk. We were in their way.

"Watch where you're going!" Jenny cried as the boys swerved around us. "You're going to ruin my dress." When the boys had passed she stood very still, inspecting every inch of her dress for a speck of dirt or a drop of mud.

"Your dress is spotless," I said gently.

"Thank goodness," Jenny replied with a big sigh.

Presently, I spied Margo and Claire Pike playing with dolls in front of their house.

"Hi, you guys," I called. "What are you up to?"

"We're playing beach," Claire answered. "See? The dirt is the sand. Our dolls are trying to get a tan."

Margo and Claire had created bikinis for the dolls by tying scraps of cloth around them. The dolls were lying on potholders. "These are their beach blankets," Margo explained.

I turned to Jenny. "Would you like to play dolls with Margo and Claire? It looks fun."

"It looks *dirty*," Jenny said, wrinkling her nose. "Look! They're sitting in the dirt like pigs." She took a few steps away from the Pikes to make sure nothing soiled her pale blue socks.

"We aren't pigs," Claire said to Margo.

"Of course not," Margo replied. "Just ignore her."

I didn't blame Margo for responding that way. Jenny had sounded pretty mean.

"We'll see you guys later," I said, taking Jenny by the hand and leading her down the sidewalk. The Pike kids didn't even say good-bye.

We reached Burnt Hill Road again and strolled over to my old street, where we spied Jamie Newton in his front yard, doing his best to master a hula hoop that was almost as big as he was. We watched him for a few minutes as, time after time, he spun the hoop and wriggled his hips frantically, trying without success to keep the plastic circle from dropping to the ground.

"You're spinning it too fast," Jenny called. "Go slower."

Jamie, who is a very sweet four-year-old, offered the hoop to Jenny. "Here," he said. "You show me how to do it."

"Ew! No!" Jenny leapt backwards as if he had thrust a snake in her face. "Get it away from me!"

I saw the puzzled look on Jamie's face and tried to explain, though I didn't really think he'd understand. "Jenny's worried the hoop might smudge her outfit."

"Oh." Jamie shrugged and, looping the hoop over his head, turned his back on Jenny. "Then I have the hula hoop all to myself."

I couldn't get over it. In less than ten minutes, Jenny had alienated six of the neighborhood kids. Our walk was turning out to be a disaster.

Making one last effort, I suggested we play on the swings at the school playground.

Jenny would have nothing to do with the idea. "Those swings are dirty and I could tear my dress."

I took a deep breath. "Then I guess we better go home."

The moment we returned to the Prezzioso house, Jenny raced to the bathroom and washed her hands. Carefully, she squeezed the soap into her palm, and then slowly scrubbed her hands. She even checked under her fingernails. (Have you ever seen a four-year-old do that? I mean, without being told to?) Just when I thought she would reach for a towel, Jenny squirted more soap on her hands and started over again. If her mother hadn't come home a few minutes later, I bet Jenny would have started a third round of washing.

I said good-bye to Jenny, promising to see her the next day. On my way home, I realized that I'd forgotten to ask Mrs. Prezzioso why she needed a sitter every weekday. I made a mental note to ask the next time. Then I thought about Jenny's strange behavior — changing her clothes for no reason, washing and rewashing her hands. It was a bit much, even for Jenny. What had gotten into her? The only thing I knew for certain was that baby-sitting for Jenny on a regular basis was going to be a real challenge.

# CHAPTER 4

Tuesday was almost an exact repeat of Monday. Once again, Miss Priss answered the doorbell. She wore a starched blue dress with a white pinafore, which tied in a big bow at the back. In her hair was a matching ribbon. I had to admit, she looked awfully sweet.

"Come on in," Jenny said, gesturing politely to the living room.

"Thanks, Jenny." I sat on the couch, and Jenny sat on a straight backed chair, taking extra care not to wrinkle her dress.

Before I could think of anything to say, Mrs. Prezzioso breezed into the room carrying Andrea, who looked like a little doll in a peach colored bonnet and dress. "Sorry I can't chat," she said. "But we must run. Here's the number where we can be reached."

She handed me a piece of paper. The number was different from the one the day before, I noticed. Mrs. Prezzioso blew a kiss to Jenny.

"Good-bye, my angel. We'll be back soon."

The moment the door was closed, I heard Jenny gasp. "Oh, no."

"What's the matter?" I asked, hurrying to her side.

Jenny pointed to a minuscule spot on her white apron. "I must have spilled my lunch!" She hopped off the chair and ran to the staircase. I thought I heard her say, "I hope Mommy didn't see."

I followed Jenny to her room. "You're not going to change your clothes again, are you?"

"I have to." Jenny sorted nervously through the dresses hanging in her closet. "This outfit is dirty now."

"Why don't you change into that?" I pointed over Jenny's shoulder to a jean jumper hanging in the far corner of her closet. "Then we can go outside and play."

Jenny stared at me as if I were crazy. "That dress makes me look ugly."

She finally chose a pink dress with puffed sleeves and a big pocket in the shape of a kitten. It was pretty. But it wasn't something anyone would wear for play.

I watched Jenny gently place it on the bed. However, instead of changing into the dress, she whirled around and scooted out the door. When I caught up with her, she was at the bathroom sink again, washing her hands.

"Are you afraid of germs?" I asked as she carefully rinsed the soap away. Maybe one of her preschool teachers had been making a big deal about handwashing. "Cold season is really almost over, you know."

Jenny made sure she dried every drop of water with the bathroom towel. "No, I just don't want to get any smudge prints on my new dress. Then I'd have to change again."

I frowned. This was not normal behavior for a four-year-old — even a super-prissy one like Jenny. It was time to get out of the house and away from the closet and that bathroom sink.

"Look, Jenny." Back in her bedroom, I pointed to her window. Outside a group of kids were huddled around Adam Pike, who was holding a clipboard. "It looks like something fun is happening."

Jenny joined me at the window. "There's Matt and Haley Braddock," she said. "And Becca Ramsey."

"Come on," I said. "Let's see what's going on."

Jenny followed me down the stairs and out the front door. (But not without checking her hair in the hall mirror.) She walked very slowly, taking care not to touch or step on anything that might spoil her outfit. We crossed the street and walked to where the kids had gathered. I arrived first, because

Jenny was gingerly picking her way around two mud puddles.

"Hey, guys," I called. "What's happening?"

Adam held up the clipboard and said, "We're organizing a neighborhood kickball team."

"Yeah," Jordan added. "It's just like Kristy's Krushers, only *we're* in charge. Not baby-sitters."

"Oh, I see," I said, remembering the triplets' declaration of independence.

Adam turned to the group of kids. "Okay. We're going to have special kicking and pitching practice. Byron will be in charge of that. Jordan will handle running and I'm the organizer. If you want to be on the team, talk to me."

I pulled Jenny aside. "Jenny, this sounds like a lot of fun. Remember when you ran in the Mini-olympics? You liked that. Why don't you sign up?"

Jenny hesitated for a second, watching the small crowd of kids gathered around Adam. She seemed pretty interested. "But I don't know how to play."

"It doesn't matter," I said. "You can learn. That's what practice is for."

"I'm not a runner," she continued. "Jordan will probably want fast runners."

"You might be a really good kicker or

pitcher. But you'll never know unless you try."

I was pushing Jenny awfully hard, but I had this idea that joining a team and playing with the other kids might take her mind off her personal war against dirt and messiness.

"Well . . ."

"Go on, Jenny," I said. "Talk to Adam. I bet you'll like it."

"Okay." Jenny took a deep breath and smoothed out the skirt of her dress. "Adam," she said, taking a big step forward. "May I please be on your kickball team?"

I couldn't believe my ears when a chorus of "no's" answered her.

"You can't let her on the team," Buddy Barrett said. "She's afraid of getting dirty."

"She'll be too fussy and she won't want to touch the ball," Nicky Pike added.

"I am not fussy," Jenny shot back.

"You are too," Margo replied. "You don't like dirt. You said so yourself."

"Stop arguing," Haley Braddock said. "I want to have fun."

"We will have fun!" Adam shouted, trying to be heard over their complaints.

"How can we have fun with her on the team?" Buddy asked, pointing at Jenny.

I was proud of Jenny; she didn't cry. I know I would have. My face would have turned beet

37

red and I would have burst into tears and probably felt as if I'd never be able to face any of those kids again. But Jenny just stood there, ignoring Buddy and Nicky and Margo, waiting for the triplets' answer.

Hmmmm. I wondered. How were the triplets going to handle this?

Adam looked at Byron, who looked at Jordan, who looked back at Adam. Finally Adam said, "Uh, don't worry, Jenny. We'll work it out."

"How?" Buddy asked.

A car horn sounded from down the street. Mrs. Prezzioso's car was turning into the driveway. Jenny didn't wait for Adam to reply. "Come on, Mary Anne," she said anxiously. Jenny made a quick check of her appearance, then hurried toward her house, once again being careful to avoid any mud puddles, twigs, or loose gravel.

Saved by the honk, I thought, glancing over my shoulder at the kids, who were still arguing about Jenny and the kickball team. I didn't know how Adam was planning to work things out, but I decided not to worry about it. I was a lot more concerned about Jenny and her new obsession with her appearance.

That night at my house, Sharon made dinner. The main course was what she calls her Health Loaf, which is like meatloaf without the meat. It's made with walnuts, carrots, zucchini, and tomatoes. I know it doesn't sound good, but it's actually kind of tasty.

"Dad?" I asked as we were finishing our dessert of chocolate chip cookies (which I had made). "What do you know about behavior problems?"

"Do you mean criminal behavior?" Dad asked. He's a lawyer in Stamford, and is always thinking like a lawyer.

"No." I wasn't sure if I wanted to tell him about Jenny in particular, so I made my question more general. "Behavior problems, like people who have to do things exactly the same way every time, or people who do things over and over, like, say, washing their hands."

"Hmmm." He scratched his chin. "Is this for a class in school?"

I shook my head. "I'm just curious."

"Well, I wouldn't say I'm an expert on those kinds of problems, but it sounds as though you're talking about obsessive behavior. I have a few psychology textbooks left over from my college days. If you want to look something up, you can borrow them."

After dinner and the dishes, I shut myself in my dad's office and stacked his psychology books in a pile on his desk. I spent the evening reading through them, and what I found was pretty scary. Many of the books described behavior like Jenny's handwashing as a symptom of a "deep-seated emotional disturbance."

An emotional disturbance? Why? Jenny seemed to have a happy home life. She'd had a little trouble getting used to her new baby sister, but that was normal. All children go through that adjustment. Besides, that was a while ago. Now she loves Andrea. What could the problem be?

Reading Dad's books hadn't made anything clearer. It had only upset me about Jenny. What if she really did have some serious psychological problem? How would I be able to help? Should I even try to help? I was going to be spending a lot of time with Jenny and, suddenly, I wasn't sure whether I was equipped to deal with her.

# CHAPTER 5

Thursday

This was a totally un-fun day. Everyone at the Pike house was complaining, including Mal.

I'm sorry, Jessi, but I couldn't help it. The triplets didn't want to be with me and I didn't want to be with them. We were trapped.

Tell me about it! Those boys spent the entire afternoon letting us know that THEY were in charge.

Everything seemed to go wrong for Jessi Thursday afternoon, starting with the triplets' "friendly" greeting at the door.

"Oh, great," Adam muttered to his brothers. "It's *another* baby-sitter. Just what we need!"

"Hello to you, too," Jessi said. "Where's Mal?"

Byron gestured vaguely toward the living room. "Around. Looking after the babies."

Then Adam grabbed his clipboard and put on his baseball cap. "If you need us, we'll be outside organizing our kickball team."

Adam and Byron headed outside but Jordan remained. "It's *totally* our team," he said pointedly. "We're *completely* in charge."

Jessi tried to sound supportive. "Good for you."

"So we don't need any help from you," he continued, "or any other baby-sitter types."

Jessi held up her hands in defeat. "Okay, okay, I get the message. I'll leave you alone."

"Good." Then Jordan ran off to join Adam and Byron, who were already in a huddle with several neighborhood kids in the front yard.

Before Jessi could recover from her conversation with the triplets, Claire appeared with tears on her cheeks.

"No fair!" she whimpered. "It's just no fair."

Jessi squatted down to face her and said, "Tell me what's wrong, Claire."

"Adam said I'm too little to play kickball. I want to pitch and they won't let me."

Jessi wiped Claire's tears off her cheeks and smoothed back her hair. "I'm sure you can kick a ball really far, but pitching is a big responsibility."

"But why won't they let me play?"

Jessi was at a loss. She wasn't sure why. After all, this was just a neighborhood team. It wasn't as if the kids would be competing in a tournament or anything. Finally Jessi said, "Why don't we talk to Adam and the boys about this? I think they owe you an explanation."

"Good." Claire folded her arms across her chest, satisfied with Jessi's decision.

Jessi allowed herself a small sigh of relief and was immediately knocked off balance by a big, slobbery dog. Or maybe I should say a long, slobbery dog. Pow the basset hound has short stubby legs but he more than makes up for it with his big strong chest, thick tail, and deep bark.

"Pow!" Jessi cried, recovering her balance. "What are you doing inside? All the kids are outside!"

"He was vacuuming the kitchen," Claire replied.

The thought of Pow moving through the kitchen sucking up crumbs and fallen food particles like a vacuum cleaner made Jessi giggle. "Well, he should be outside. Does he know that his old owner is here?"

Pow used to belong to the Barretts, until they discovered that Marnie, the littlest Barrett, who is allergic to chocolate, is also allergic to dog dander. Buddy and Suzy were heartbroken when they found out they had to give Pow away. Luckily, the Pikes agreed to take him in. Mrs. Pike tried to make a rule that Pow was to stay outside as much as possible, but the kids didn't always enforce it.

"Don't make him go outside!" Claire pleaded. Her chin started to quiver and she looked as if she were going to cry again.

Before Jessi could answer Claire, Mallory came into the living room. She didn't look happy.

"I've had it!" she said. "I can't do anything. I'm locked in this house like a prisoner."

Jessi had been listening patiently to Mallory's complaints for weeks. "Is this about your parents?" she asked.

"Yes." Mallory shoved her glasses up on her nose with one finger. "Why won't they let me do anything? I go to school, come home, do homework — "

"And look after the kids," Jessi finished with her.

That made Mallory pause. She grinned sheepishly at Jessi. "I've said this before, right?"

Jessi gave an emphatic nod. "Yes. At least a hundred times."

Mal tilted her head and thought for a second. "Well, it just goes to show how frustrated I am."

"I *know* how frustrated you are. And I know how frustrated the triplets are. And you know what?" Jessi added. "*I'm* getting frustrated. I think being inside this house is doing it to me. I vote we go outside."

"I second the motion," Vanessa Pike said as she trotted down the stairs from her room. She and Claire were the only Pike kids still in the house. The rest were already out in the yard with the triplets.

Unfortunately, the situation didn't improve much when Mal and Jessi stepped outside. In fact, judging from all the shouting, things seemed to have gotten worse.

"You *have* to have rules!" Buddy was yelling. "If you don't, the whole team will fall apart."

"We *do* have rules," Adam shot back. "*Our* rules."

"Well, if we're going to pick sides," Buddy said, "I want to choose who's on my side."

The arguing had started when Jenny and I arrived. The triplets still hadn't decided whether they were going to let Jenny be on their team.

Mallory hurried over to see what was wrong.

"Some of the kids think Jenny might not be a good team member," I said, trying to keep my voice low so Jenny wouldn't overhear.

Mal snorted. "I'm tempted to tell those kids they *better* let her on the team."

Before she could storm away, I grabbed her by the arm and whispered, "The problem is — they may be right."

"What do you mean?"

Since Mallory was on a leave of absence from the BSC, she had missed my news about the reappearance of Miss Priss. (I'd told everybody else at Wednesday's meeting.) So I filled her in on Jenny's strange behavior.

"And I'm starting to think it has something to do with her mom and Andrea disappearing every afternoon," I concluded.

"Where do they go?" Mal asked.

"I'm not sure," I said, feeling a little foolish. "Mrs. Prezzioso always leaves a phone number where I can reach her, but she never tells me where they're headed. And here's the odd part — the telephone number changes every day."

"Why don't you just ask her where she's going?"

Mallory's question was a reasonable one but I didn't have a reasonable answer. "I know this sounds silly," I said, "but I feel like I'd be prying. Anyway, I never asked before, so it would seem kind of odd for me to ask now."

"I think you deserve an explanation from Mrs. Prezzioso," Mallory said. "I mean, if you want to help Jenny, you need to know what's going on in her life."

I shrugged helplessly. "I guess you're right. But maybe they're not connected. The only thing I'm certain of is that according to Dad's textbooks, Jenny has become an obsessive personality."

"Obsessive?" Mallory repeated. Her eyes widened.

We watched as Jenny made her way along the edge of the lawn toward the porch steps. She seemed to be eyeing each blade of grass she passed, to make sure it didn't flick dirt or water onto her tights.

"I think I see what you mean," Mallory whispered.

Suddenly Jessi, who had been trying to talk

to the triplets about Claire, threw up her hands and stalked away in disgust. "Can you believe it?" she said to Mallory and me. "They can't make up their minds about Claire or Jenny. What's the big deal?"

"Maybe we should do something," I said.

"Uh-uh." Mallory shook her head. "Adam and the boys said it's *their* team and *they're* in charge. I think we'd better let them work it out."

Jessi turned to look at the boys again. "I don't think they're going to do anything except let everyone shout at each other."

"Maybe we *should* offer some guidance." I was feeling bad for Jenny. But before I could call a halt to the bickering, Jenny, who had finally reached the porch, made her own announcement.

"Kickball is a dirty sport," she shouted from the steps. "I quit!"

"Hooray!" Buddy and a couple of other kids shouted.

Then Jenny called to me, "Mary Anne! I would like to go home now, please."

Frankly, I was glad to leave the Pike place. Too many kids were in rotten moods. I felt a little bad about leaving Jessi and Mal with all those angry children, but I figured the two of them could handle it.

"It's a good thing we're leaving," Jenny said,

pointing to her tights as we walked away. "Look at this stain. I'll have to change my clothes."

Jessi and Mallory watched us walk away and then turned to face each other. "I'm not having a very good day," Jessi said matter-of-factly. "Are you having a good day?"

Mallory shook her head miserably. "On a scale of one to ten — ten being really frustrating — I'd have to say today is a nine-and-a-half."

Jessi nodded. "Definitely not a good day."

# CHAPTER 6

Where was Mrs. Prezzioso taking Andrea every afternoon? The members of the BSC considered the possibilities. Stacey baby-sat for Jenny on Wednesday, and Claudia took the Friday slot and, each time, Mrs. Prezzioso bustled out the door, leaving the number where she could be reached on the refrigerator door but not mentioning where she was going.

Jenny was lying on the couch when I arrived on Monday afternoon. She had a headache, and Mrs. Prezzioso was afraid she might be coming down with something. Andrea, as usual, was dressed like a little doll. She sat happily on the floor of the living room while Mrs. Prezzioso took some extra time giving me instructions before they left.

"Other than her headache, Jenny doesn't have any symptoms," Mrs. Prezzioso explained. "I've given her a little Tylenol, so that should hold her. Here's where I can be reached."

Mrs. Prezzioso handed me a piece of paper with a phone number on it. The exchange was different from the numbers she had given me before. Were she and Andrea going far away? Maybe this was my chance to find out where she was headed.

"If Jenny gets really sick," I said, remembering the time she had had a terribly high temperature while I was baby-sitting and had had to be taken to the hospital, "would you be able to come quickly? I mean . . . where will you be?"

Mrs. Prezzioso pursed her lips and stared at me for a moment. Then she sat on the edge of the couch. "I've been a little reluctant to mention it, but Andrea and I have been going to auditions."

"Auditions?"

"For television commercials and print work," she explained. "You know — catalogs, advertisements, that sort of thing." She glanced over at Andrea, who was cuddling a fuzzy teddy bear, and smiled. "We've booked quite a few jobs."

I was amazed. "You mean that's where you go every day?"

Mrs. Prezzioso nodded. "Sometimes the auditions are at our agent's office, but we often go directly to the production studios. It's a rather demanding schedule."

"I didn't realize there were that many jobs for babies."

"Oh, there are. Every Sunday paper has an advertising section featuring the current sales in the big department stores. They always need models. Then there are clothing catalogues, and television commercials selling baby food, diapers, and general family items. Not to mention all the products that use babies in their ads just for humor, like those tire commercials. Sometimes Andrea and I are on the road all day — mornings, too — just going from one audition or job to another."

Mrs. Prezzioso was trying to sound very businesslike, but I could tell she was bubbling over with pride at how well her beautiful baby was doing.

Jenny had been quiet while her mother spoke. Finally she said, "Mommy, could I please go to the audition with you today? I promise I'll be good. I'll sit very still while you're in the studio and I won't say a word."

I realized that Jenny had probably already gone along on a few auditions, at times when Mrs. Prezzioso couldn't find a sitter.

"Please, Mommy? Oh, please, oh, please!"

Mrs. Prezzioso seemed touched by Jenny's interest. "Well . . . all right," she said. "If Mary Anne comes with us."

I agreed. I thought it would be fun to see how actors are chosen for commercials. Maybe I'd even see someone famous!

Jenny made a miraculous recovery from her headache. She was standing by the front door before the rest of us had a chance to move. And she was so happy to be with her mother and sister that she burst into song the moment the car pulled out of the driveway.

"The wheels on the bus go round and round, round and round, round and round, the wheels on the bus go round and round, all through the town."

We sang all the verses of the song, including the ones about the baby crying, and the mother shushing it. Andrea giggled with delight and clapped her hands (though not exactly on the beat).

The talent agent's office was in another town on this side of Stamford. I spotted it right away. I could see a steady stream of mothers and babies heading toward the big glass doors of an ultra-modern building.

We pulled into the parking lot and Jenny stopped singing. She knew it was time to get down to business. She sat quietly as Mrs. Prezzioso brushed Andrea's hair and retied her bonnet, smoothed out Andrea's tights and checked her hands to make sure they were spotless. No wonder Jenny was such a clean fiend. She learned it from her mother.

The Tip-Top Talent Agency's offices were in the penthouse of the building. The four of us rode up in an elevator packed with other children and their moms or dads. It was a bizarre ride. The children didn't act like regular kids at all.

Most stood quietly. One little girl, who looked five but sounded more like fifteen, was giving her mother instructions. "Now when they call my name, I want to go by myself. They like it better when I'm alone. Okay, Mother?"

Her mother, a tired-looking woman in a rumpled blue suit, nodded. "Fine, dear. I'll stay in the waiting room."

The doors opened into a huge carpeted waiting room filled with black-and-white striped couches and lots of big plants. Framed pictures of magazine ads and movie posters covered the walls.

"We have to check in," Mrs. Prezzioso said. "Why don't you two find a place for us to sit?"

I looked around the crowded room and wondered silently, where? The couches were taken, and the corners were filled with mothers and fathers clutching pieces of paper as they read dialogue with their kids. I chose a not-so-crowded corner for us. Mrs. Prezzioso explained that the slips of paper weren't the full script, but only the kid's parts. "They're called sides," she added.

I love being around kids, but watching this group gave me a weird feeling. None of them was playing. In fact, some of the children sat stiff as little automatons while their parents murmured instructions in their ears. Every now and then they would nod, without even looking at their mothers or fathers.

A woman named Joan, with bright red hair, big horn-rimmed glasses, dangling earrings, and a layered black outfit appeared at the receptionist's desk. She held a clipboard in one hand. "Katie Collins, Kirk Enquist, Millicent Montague, and Tiffany Wells," she announced in a loud voice. "You're up."

"Excuse me." A distraught mother hurried to Joan. "Millicent really does better in a one-on-one situation," she said. "Those other children, especially Tiffany Wells, will get in the way."

Joan shrugged. "Millicent auditions with the other kids, or she doesn't audition at all. Those are the rules."

After a few final instructions from their parents, the four children whose names had been called filed through a door into another room. I got a glimpse of the room as Joan held the door open. It looked like a dance studio, with a shiny wood floor and lots of mirrors. Several adults were seated behind a long table at the far side of the room.

After the door closed, the receptionist, who looked like a model herself, made a general announcement. "When the kids are done, they'll be seeing babies for the Yummy Tummy spot. If you'd like to look at the storyboard, I have it here at my desk."

"What's a storyboard?" I whispered to Mrs. Prezzioso.

"It shows what the television commercial will look like," Jenny replied.

Mrs. Prezzioso smiled at Jenny. "That's right, angel. It goes through the spot, frame by frame."

Along with some other moms and babies, we walked up to the reception desk and looked at a piece of art board covered with rows of pictures, like a comic strip. "Here's a close-up of the product, and this is a long shot. You see?" Mrs. Prezzioso pointed to one of the squares. "It shows the baby and the whole room. In this case the Yummy Tummy spot is basically about a baby eating Grandma Perkins Apple Dumpling baby food and getting it everywhere."

I had to laugh. The artist had drawn a baby holding a spoon in one hand and rubbing her stomach with the other. Her face, nose, bib, and the entire kitchen seemed to be covered with blobs of baby food.

"How will Andrea audition for that?" I asked.

"Oh, they'll probably put a bib on her and hand her a spoon, and then videotape whatever happens," Mrs. Prezzioso replied. "Andrea loves the camera. As soon as she sees that red light, she comes alive."

The receptionist, whose nameplate read Libby, squeezed the toe of Andrea's bootie. "And how does Miss Andrea feel about Grandma's apple dumplings?"

Andrea answered with a bubbly giggle and a clap of her hands, which made everyone laugh.

"She's adorable," Libby said with a sigh to Mrs. Prezzioso. "An absolute doll."

I caught the expression on Jenny's face when Libby said that. She drooped. As we returned to our corner, several mothers stopped us to coo over Andrea.

"What a little princess," one mother said. "And so well-behaved. Does she ever cry?"

Mrs. Prezzioso shook her head. "Almost never."

A woman sitting nearby looked up from the

magazine she was reading. "Yes, little Andrea is the darling of the industry." She sounded bitter. "Why, I'll bet she books nearly as many commercials as she auditions for."

"One out of three," Mrs. Prezzioso replied coolly.

I felt a little confused by all the show biz talk. "What does book mean?"

"It means that you've been hired for the job." Mrs. Prezzioso hugged Andrea, who was examining the ribbon of her bonnet. "And Andrea is hired for quite a few jobs."

I checked Jenny's reaction. Again, she looked terribly sad. But she quickly put on a smile and patted Andrea on the back. "My sister is perfect."

So that was it. Andrea was perfect, and Andrea got heaps of attention. Andrea was a baby star who made TV commercials, and modeled for magazines, and was showered with compliments from total strangers, while Jenny was just a regular little girl. She was feeling left out, and she'd decided that the best way to get some attention for herself was to be just as neat, clean, and perfect as her sister.

The door from the studio burst open and the girl named Millicent ran into the room, followed by Joan. "Mommy!" she cried. "I want to go home. They're a bunch of meanies."

"What's the matter, dear?" Mrs. Montague cried, rushing to her daughter's side.

Joan fixed Mrs. Montague with a stare. "We asked her to eat some of Grandma's Kiddie Casserole and she refused. She said it made her want to throw up."

"Millicent has a very delicate stomach," her mother replied.

Joan blew out her cheeks in frustration. "Why didn't you tell us that before the audition? You and your daughter have just wasted a great deal of precious time."

"Come on, Millie," said her mother huffily, ushering her daughter toward the elevator doors. "We don't have to listen to her. That Grandma's kiddie food is terrible. I wouldn't have been able to eat it either."

The director's assistant didn't seem to be fazed by Mrs. Montague's comment. She shook her head, and then checked her clipboard. "All right, folks. It's baby time and Andrea Prezzioso is on deck."

While Jenny and I waited for Andrea to audition, I wondered what I would do in Jenny's position. Would I try to compete with my sister, the way Jenny was doing, or would I just give up and get depressed? That was something to discuss with my friends. I couldn't wait for our Monday afternoon BSC meeting. We had a *lot* to talk about.

"So the mystery is solved," Claudia said. Our Monday afternoon meeting had begun, and she was passing around a bowl of potato chips and pretzels. "We finally know where Mrs. Prezzioso and Andrea have been going."

"The mystery is solved," I said, taking a handful of chips, "but not the problem. Jenny's still Miss Priss. She's going overboard staying clean and neat because she's trying to compete with Andrea. She's heard so many people call Andrea perfect, she's starting to believe it — and to believe that looking perfect is the only way she'll get any attention for herself, I think."

Stacey dug in the bowl and pulled out a pretzel. "I had no idea the Prezziosos wanted to be in show business."

"Mrs. Prezzioso does seem like the perfect stage mother," Jessi said. She's met more than one in the dance world, I guess.

"And remember how competitive she got when Andrea was in the baby parade?" Kristy added.

I frowned. "I wish Jenny would realize that she's beautiful, too, and lots of fun to be around. I can see why it's hard, though. People are always going to make a bigger fuss over a baby who giggles and coos than an older kid."

Everyone nodded. We sat quietly, trying to think of a way to let Jenny know she was just as important and wonderful as Andrea.

*Brrring!*

The phone broke the silence so abruptly that we jumped.

"Yipes!" Claud shrieked.

All of us giggled, but Kristy laughed so hard that potato chips exploded out of her mouth. That did it. Nobody could answer the phone.

*Brrring!*

"You get it," Kristy managed to gasp. She pointed at Stacey.

Stacey couldn't even talk. She was laughing so hard that tears were streaming down her face. She just shook her head and pointed at Claudia.

Claudia stopped snickering long enough to yelp, "No way, José!" She motioned at me to pick up the phone, and her gesture knocked the bowl of chips onto the carpet. Of course, that made us laugh even harder.

*Brrring!*

This was getting bad. A client was calling and no one was answering. We gulped deep breaths of air, trying desperately to compose ourselves. Shannon recovered first and dove for the phone before it could ring again.

"Baby-sitters Club, this is Shannon Kilbourne," she said in an ultra-formal voice, which set us all off again.

"Oh, hello, Mrs. Prezzioso," Shannon said, looking meaningfully at the group. Instantly, we quieted. "Yes, she's here," Shannon replied. "Would you like to speak to her?"

Shannon held the phone toward me. I put the receiver to my ear, hoping nothing was wrong.

"Hi, Mrs. Prezzioso," I said. "Is Jenny all right?"

"Oh, she's fine. In fact, she's more than fine. She's decided she would like to be a model, just like Andrea."

Surprise, surprise. "Really!"

"And she seems to be very serious about it."

"I think Jenny would make a wonderful model," I said sincerely.

I saw the other members of the BSC, who were obviously listening to my side of the conversation, raise their eyebrows at each other.

"Why, thank you," Mrs. Prezzioso replied. "Anyway, I've made an appointment for Jenny to have some head shots taken — "

"Head shots?" It sounded like some painful medical procedure.

"Photos for her portfolio," Mrs. Prezzioso explained. "All models and actors need them. I'm sending her to Robert Gautier's studio on Thursday. He did Andrea's head shots. He's wonderful."

"That's great." I shrugged at the group. I wasn't sure why Mrs. Prezzioso was telling me all of this.

"But I have a problem," she continued. "Andrea got a callback for a national spot at the time of Jenny's photo session. I really can't cancel, since Robert is usually booked up weeks in advance. Would you mind staying with Jenny at the photo session while I take Andrea to the callback?"

Usually, when a client calls, we take down the information and then discuss it with the other BSC members to see who is available. But since I'd agreed to be Jenny's semi-permanent sitter, I told Mrs. Prezzioso I'd do it.

"You're an absolute dear," Mrs. Prezzioso said. "I'll see you at three-thirty sharp on Thursday."

I hung up, and promptly filled my friends in on what Mrs. Prezzioso had said.

"Jenny is a natural for commercials," Kristy said thoughtfully. "I'm surprised she didn't think of it before."

Claudia, who had managed to scoop most of the chips and pretzels back in the bowl and was now licking the salt off her fingertips, said, "This should solve Jenny's problem. She and Andrea will both be successful models, so no more competing for attention."

"You know, I'm not so sure about that," I said, biting my lower lip anxiously. "I mean, what if she *isn't* a success? Just because you're pretty doesn't mean you automatically get the job."

I worried about Jenny for the rest of the meeting and on and off over the next three days. On Thursday, Mrs. Prezzioso drove us to Robert Gautier's as planned. His studio was in this really wonderful old Victorian house.

The front parlor was stuffed with antiques and oriental rugs. It was gorgeous, but it looked inviting, too — not like a museum. Dressing rooms were under the stairs. While Mrs. Prezzioso checked in with the receptionist, I carried Jenny's bags in from the car.

She had so much luggage, it looked as if we were moving in. I'm not kidding. I brought in a garment bag that held five changes of clothes for Jenny, a canvas tote filled with five pairs of shoes, a small overnight case holding brushes, face powder, hair ribbons, and gloves, and a shopping bag loaded with props — a plush teddy bear, a doll, and a stack of beautifully illustrated storybooks.

While I struggled to fit everything into one of the dressing rooms, Jenny nervously checked and re-checked her appearance in the hall mirror.

"All right, my angel. I've arranged everything," Mrs. Prezzioso announced. "Just do what Mr. Gautier tells you and don't forget to smile. We're sure to get some lovely shots for your portfolio."

I held Andrea so that Mrs. Prezzioso could hug Jenny. It wasn't much of a hug. They both seemed overly concerned about mussing Jenny's hair and clothes.

"Is there anything special you want me to do?" I asked Mrs. Prezzioso as she headed for the door.

"Just keep Jenny calm and I'll see you in an hour."

Calm? That would be a challenge. Jenny knew this afternoon's session was a big deal, and she was nervous. To make matters worse, we had a ten-minute wait ahead of us. Jenny tried her hardest to sit still but ten minutes can be an eternity for a four year old. I tried to play a quiet game with her, but she couldn't concentrate. She squirmed in her chair. Then she paced the room. She checked the mirror.

Finally, Robert Gautier strode into the room, looking as if he had just stepped off the deck of a cruise ship. He wore crisp white pants and a white polo shirt that showed off his incredible tan. Resting in his jet-black hair was a pair of designer sunglasses.

"Jen?" he asked, flashing Jenny a smile. "You ready?"

Jenny snapped to attention. "Yes I am."

"Call me Bob," he said, as he steered her toward the dressing room. "Now let's take a look at your wardrobe."

I followed them and was very impressed at how professional Jenny acted. She unzipped the garment bag and Bob mm-hmmed over her dresses. Finally he turned to Jenny, and took a long look at her face, tapping his chin thoughtfully.

"I think the dress you're wearing is a very good choice," Bob declared. "We'll start with that."

I introduced myself to Bob as we followed him into the studio, explaining that I was Jenny's baby-sitter.

"Jen doesn't need a sitter, do you?" Bob teased as he gestured for Jenny to sit on a big black laminated cube. "You're much too grown up."

Bob's studio had white walls, with huge

lights hanging from the ceiling and smaller ones set on tripods. Sheets of shiny thin metal, for reflecting more light, I figured, surrounded what was clearly the modeling area. Bob spent the next few minutes trying out different backdrops. First he lowered a sheet of blue wrinkled canvas to the floor.

Bob studied it for a few minutes and finally said, "Nope. All wrong." Eventually he settled on a pale gray canvas drop that was spotted with black and white globs of paint. "Yes!"

Jenny tried to sit patiently as he adjusted the lights and reflectors, but this took a lot of time. Without thinking, she started kicking her heels against the cube in a *thud-thud*, *thud-thud* rhythm.

"Jen." Bob raised an eyebrow at her and said, "That's a lovely beat you've got there, but perhaps we could continue it later."

Jenny's eyes widened. "Sorry," she said in a timid voice.

He took lots of shots of her, some with a hand-held camera and some with a big camera on a tripod. After a while he changed the backdrop. Otherwise, every shot seemed pretty much the same.

"Tilt your chin down. Thatta girl. Look over here. Can you give us a smile?"

Jenny tried to follow directions, but even I felt a little confused with all of the chin down, eyes up, straight back, and look over here stuff.

"All right," Bob said at last. "Let's take a break. I think it's time for a different outfit. Why don't you change into the lavender one. And maybe we'll use a prop this time."

The minute Jenny and I were in the dressing room, she turned to me and whispered, "Am I doing okay?"

I hugged her, making sure not to touch her hair. "You're doing more than okay, you're doing great. You look like a real model up there."

Jenny changed quickly into her lavender outfit. We retouched her hair and then grabbed the bag of props and brought them with us. Bob was drinking a can of Coke and talking on his portable phone when we returned.

"No," we heard him say. "The fifteenth is out. I'm completely booked till the twentieth and then it's back to the Bahamas for those cruise shots." (Hmm. So that's where he got the tan.)

While Jenny and I waited for him to finish his call, she stifled a yawn. Being a model was tiring.

Suddenly, Bob appeared beside us, wearing a silly black hat with long, floppy dog ears dangling from either side. "Okay, Jen," he said in a Goofy voice. "We're going to have some fun now!"

Bob really was being funny, and Jenny tried her best to be lively and cute, first cuddling the teddy bear for the camera, then posing with her doll. After that, Bob decided he wanted pictures of Jenny and the bear and doll having a tea party. He lowered a backdrop painted to look like the interior of a wonderful old house, with flowered wall paper and a window with a spotted geranium on the sill.

It took quite a while to set up the tea party. And even though Bob was chatting and joking all the while, it was starting to look as though the bear and the doll were having a much better time than Jenny was. She was starting to droop.

"How you doing, Jen?" Bob asked as he reloaded his camera.

"I'm fine, Mr. Gautier," she replied. "I mean, Mr. Bob — I mean . . ." Her voice trailed off and I saw her chin start to quiver.

That's when I stepped forward. "I think Jenny could use something to drink."

Bob gestured to the refrigerator at the far end of the room. "Help yourself to some juice or soda," he said, with a sympathetic smile. "I know she's getting a little tired, but we're almost through." He turned to Jenny. "Can you hold out a little longer?"

Jenny nodded solemnly. I found a can of apple juice in the refrigerator and Jenny took a couple of sips, being careful (of course) not to spill anything on herself.

"For the final series," Bob said, "let's play a game I call The Robot. I'll give you instructions, and you do exactly what I say. Sound like fun?"

I thought it sounded terrible, but Jenny tried to look enthusiastic. For this shot, Bob raised all of the curtain drops and posed Jenny in front of the bare white walls.

"Ready?" He put the camera up to his eye and aimed it at Jenny. "Now walk. That's good. Now stop. Turn. Look at me. Smile. Cock your head. Turn and walk. Look up. Stop. Look at me."

It was like a giant game of Simon Says. Jenny did her best to obey his commands, but unfortunately she looked too much like a robot, stopping stiffly, and grimacing as she concentrated on making every turn.

"All right, Jen," Bob said, arranging her on the pedestal one last time. "I want you to face the camera and say — "

Bob whispered something in her ear and the biggest and brightest smile of the afternoon spread across Jenny's face. She looked directly into the camera and shouted gleefully, *"The end!"*

Boy, was she glad that was over! Me, too. That afternoon, I realized something that I had not known before. Modeling is *very* hard work.

# CHAPTER 8

Jenny's pictures came out great. But guess which shot was the very best? The one Bob snapped when Jenny shouted, "The end!"

Mrs. Prezzioso wasted no time. She had copies printed up right away, and rushed them over to the Tip Top Talent Agency, who started sending the photos out. Exactly one week later, Jenny landed an audition for Karbergers department store in Hartford. They were starting a new television campaign, and planned to run related ads in the newspapers. Karbergers wanted children of all ages, so Andrea was called, too. The audition was scheduled for a Thursday, one of my regular sitting days, so I went along to help Mrs. Prezzioso out.

The auditions were being held at the offices of the department store, on the eighth floor of their building. Andrea was still napping when we got out of the car in the parking garage. We decided to leave her in her car seat and take it to the audition.

What a zoo! At least fifty people were crammed into a small waiting room outside the marketing director's office. With that many bodies in such a small space, the temperature had skyrocketed. People were cranky. Babies were crying. Kids pleaded with their parents to leave, while the mothers and fathers complained to each other, loudly.

"This is no way to run an audition," one woman was saying. "You can't call this many children at once and expect a good performance. The kids will get squirrelly."

"The *kids*?" a man repeated. He was wedged into a corner with his two-year-old son. "It's the parents I'm concerned about. I've only been here fifteen minutes and already I've heard two mothers completely lose it."

Mrs. Prezzioso picked up copies of the script at the desk, then made her way through the crowd to the small patch of floor space Jenny and I had staked out.

"Shall we go over your part, angel?" Mrs. Prezzioso asked Jenny.

"I can't read," she said in dismay.

Mrs. Prezzioso laughed. "Don't worry, I'll tell you the words and you can memorize them."

The door to the hall outside swung open

just then, and another group of children and parents crowded into the office. The noise level rose a few notches.

"Why don't we wait in the hall?" I suggested to Mrs. Prezzioso.

She shook her head emphatically. "If we wait out there, we could get passed over. The casting director likes to see the talent. We need to be right here, in front of her face."

With that, Mrs. Prezzioso dropped to her knees and gestured for me to hand her Andrea, who was still snoozing in her car seat. Jenny and I wedged ourselves between a woman with one-year-old twins and a grandmother and her five-year-old grandson, who looked like a miniature baseball player. He wore a uniform and even carried a small bat and glove.

"Now, Jenny, the first spot is a happy one. All you have to do is smile and say, 'Mommy, let's always go to Karbergers. They're the best!' Can you do that?"

Jenny nodded. "I think so."

"Then try it."

Jenny took a deep breath, didn't smile, and said "Mommy I want to go to Kar . . . um, Kar . . . Kar . . ."

She'd forgotten the name of the store. The boy in the baseball outfit leaned over and said, in a matter-of-fact voice, "The store's name is

Karbergers — like hamburger, with a car in front of it."

Mrs. Prezzioso smiled. "That young man is right. And, honey, you need to pronounce the name of the store correctly. Keep repeating it: Karbergers, Karbergers, Karbergers."

Jenny scowled as she concentrated. "Karbergers, Karberg — "

"Don't frown," Mrs. Prezzioso coached Jenny. "You're supposed to be happy. Remember? Karbergers makes you happy."

"It does?" Jenny asked vaguely. She was definitely losing interest in the happy Karbergers spot. And starting to get the fidgets.

Mrs. Prezzioso made a decision. "Okay. Forget the happy commercial. Let's just concentrate on the second one. In this spot you're supposed to be very sad and pout and say, 'I want to go to Karbergers.' "

"Do you still want me to smile?" Jenny asked.

Mrs. Prezzioso blew a strand of hair off her forehead in frustration. "No, you're sad now. What do you do when you're sad?"

"Cry?"

"Exactly!"

Jenny and I stared at Mrs. Prezzioso.

"You want Jenny to cry?" I asked in amazement.

"*I* don't," Mrs. Prezzioso replied. "The department store people do. When the little girl in this commercial sees what an inferior product the competitor has provided, she bursts into tears and begs her mommy to take her to Karbergers."

Jenny squeezed her face into an ugly grimace but nothing happened. "Do you see any tears?" she whispered to me out of the side of her mouth.

"Not yet," I whispered back. "But I'm sure you can manage to squeeze out a few. Why don't you try saying the line at the same time? Maybe it will make you feel sad."

"I forgot it," Jenny said miserably. "What is it, Mommy?"

"*I want to go to Karbergers!*" a little girl across the room wailed at the top of her lungs.

The room instantly fell silent as everybody, parents and children, realized *that* was the way the line should be read. Lots of urgent whispering followed. Soon, "I want to go to Karbergers!" was being bellowed from every corner of the room. Jenny tried to join in, but her effort wasn't very convincing.

Eventually, several of the babies in the room got scared and added some *real* crying to the din. The place sounded like an out-of-control nursery. Here's what's amazing — Andrea slept peacefully through it all.

Jenny covered her ears with her hands.

"Mommy, my ears hurt. Tell them to be quiet."

"I can't, darling," Mrs. Prezzioso said, raising her voice to be heard over the wailing. "They're practicing, which is what you should do if you want to get that part."

A woman stuck her head out of the inner office and shouted, "Quiet, please! We can't hear ourselves think!"

That shut everyone up — except the babies. The waiting seemed endless. Jenny got the fidgets again. She couldn't seem to find a comfortable position. First she knelt. Then she sat cross-legged. Then she stood. Then she wanted to go to the bathroom, so I took her. Just as we returned, the casting director came out of the inner office and asked for everyone's attention.

She was very different from the woman at the last audition. Her name tag read Carolyn DeVries. Ms. DeVries wore a navy blue linen suit with navy blue heels. Her collar-length blonde hair seemed to be glued in place like a helmet. Ms. DeVries glanced at her watch and announced, "We're running behind."

"No kidding!" a sarcastic voice muttered from the couch. I didn't turn around but I had a feeling it was the lady who had been complaining when we first arrived.

"We've decided to line up the talent for the

crying spot and videotape them all at once. We'll do individual reads in callbacks."

"Oh, great," the man in the corner groaned. "It's a free for all."

"All right," Ms. DeVries said. "All children reading for the 'I want to go to Karbergers' spot,' line up here." She drew an imaginary line on the carpet with the toe of her high heel.

It seemed as though everyone in the room stood up. Ms. DeVries held up her hands. "No parents, please! There's just no room for you."

"But my son is shy when he meets strangers," one father said, hugging his little boy. "Couldn't I please come in with him?"

Ms. DeVries was polite but firm. "I'm sorry, sir, but the room is just too small. It's also very important for us to cast children who can handle being alone."

Mrs. Prezzioso whispered to Jenny, "How do you feel? Can you do this by yourself?"

Jenny nodded tensely.

"Good. Then line up with the other children. And remember, the store's name is Karbergers."

Jenny stared straight ahead and mumbled, "Karbergers. Karbergers."

Ms. DeVries smiled at the row of waiting kids. "All right, children, follow me."

As I watched Jenny and the other kids file

into the marketing director's office, I felt butterflies in my stomach, as if I were auditioning, too. It was a horrible feeling.

"What happens to Jenny now?" I asked Mrs. Prezzioso.

"They're lining the children up in front of the director and clients," she explained. "Then one by one they'll ask each child to state her name and her agent's name for the camera. That's called slating your name. After that, they'll ask the children to cry."

"Are there really kids who can cry on cue?" I asked.

"Oh, yes," Mrs. Prezzioso said. "That little girl in the corner was quite good, but one of the best of them was sitting right next to us. The little boy in the baseball uniform? He's a great crier and laugher. He's always booked."

I shook my head. "What a strange way to make a living."

"Actually it's not usually a living," Mrs. Prezzioso replied. "The money our girls make from these commercials will go directly into their college fund. The same is true for many of the other children here."

The door to the office opened and the children paraded back into the room. Jenny knelt beside me and stared down at the carpet. She didn't say a word.

"We're looking at babies now," Ms. DeVries announced.

"Waaaa!" A very grouchy baby behind us started to cry and Ms. DeVries arched one eyebrow. "Happy babies, please. We don't need tears for this spot."

"Well, what do you expect?" the baby's mother snapped. "We're crammed into this stuffy room and forced to wait forever. It would be a miracle if the children didn't cry."

Ms. DeVries ignored the lady's remark and quickly scanned the room. "I'll see you, and you, and you." She pointed at several mothers holding babies in their arms. "And this little sleepyhead here." She smiled at Andrea, who was still snoozing in her car seat.

Mrs. Prezzioso stood up. "You and Jenny wait here and we'll be back soon."

When Mrs. Prezzioso and Andrea had left, I asked Jenny gently, "How'd it go?"

Jenny still didn't look up from the carpet. Her lower lip trembled as she said, "Not very good. I forgot the store's name. I said Hamburgers."

"Oh, Jenny!" I swallowed a laugh and gave her a great big hug. "*I've* been calling them Hamburgers for years. It's okay. Everybody does it."

Jenny looked at me in surprise. "Really?"

I crossed my heart and held up one hand. "I promise."

The babies' audition was much shorter than the one with older kids. Andrea was awake and smiling when they reappeared.

"You were wonderful!" Mrs. Prezzioso was nuzzling Andrea's cheek. "You let everyone hold you and you didn't cry once!"

The casting director, who had followed them through the door, put her hand on Mrs. Prezzioso's shoulder and said, "This one is a perfect darling. We'll see her again on Saturday."

"What about me?" Jenny spoke up. "Would you like me to come, too?"

Ms. DeVries looked at Jenny. "No, dear. We won't need to see you again. But thank you for coming."

Jenny's shoulders slumped and I could see that she was struggling to hold back tears.

We rode to Stoneybrook in silence. Neither Mrs. Prezzioso nor I could get Jenny to sing one song. I didn't blame her for feeling so glum. I would have felt miserable, too.

# CHAPTER 9

Monday

I never knew kickball could be such a wild game. I sat for the Barretts today and watched a neighborhood match. The Pike triplets were in charge— at least that's what they kept telling everybody. But it sure didn't seem like it....

Shannon is a stickler for rules. Watching the kids trying to work out the guidelines for their kickball team must have made her crazy. It was Monday, and I was with the Prezziosos at an audition for a toy commercial. The Pikes' kickball game was scheduled to take place at Brenner Field at exactly four o'clock. Most of the BSC was in attendance. Claudia was in charge of the Braddock kids, Jessi was watching her sister Becca, and Mallory (who had to promise she'd sit quietly) and Stacey were Pike-sitting.

"We're going to divide the team into two groups," Adam announced as Shannon and the Barretts arrived.

"I want to be on Buddy's team," Nicky Pike shouted.

"Me too," Suzi Barrett cried.

"Becca Ramsey and I have to be on the same team," Haley Braddock declared.

"I want to be with Haley and Becca!" Margo shouted.

Adam waved his hands in the air. "Quiet! Quiet, everybody! *We'll* pick the teams and you have to do what we say."

"Why?" Buddy asked.

"Because this is *our* team," Jordan replied. "And what we say goes, or else."

Jordan's answer caused some grumbling in

the group. Suzi Barrett nudged her brother. "He can't act that way. Can he?"

Buddy shrugged and muttered, "I don't think so."

Shannon, who was sitting on the grass with Marnie, turned to Mallory and Stacey. "It looks like those guys are heading for a big argument. Should we say something?"

"No!" Stacey and Mallory replied together.

"The triplets have made it very clear to all of us that this is their team," Stacey explained, "and that they don't need any help or advice from anyone." She rolled her eyes and added, "Especially not the BSC."

"Okay," Shannon said. "But this is not the best way to start a game. They haven't even picked teams yet."

Adam blew the whistle hanging around his neck. "Okay. The girls against the boys."

"No!" Byron folded his arms across his chest. "That's no good. It's an uneven number."

"Well, then you choose the teams," Adam snapped. "But hurry up."

Byron took a deep breath. "Count off. All the even numbers will be on one team and the odds on the other."

The kids counted off and then split into two groups.

"Well, I'm glad that's over," Shannon said

with a sigh. "Now let's see how they do in the game."

The game was a disaster. First, Haley insisted on being the pitcher. The problem was, Adam and Jordan were on her team, and they wanted to pitch, too. But Haley stood firm.

"If I don't pitch, I'm quitting," she said. "And the rest of the girls will probably quit, too."

Finally Adam gave up. "Oh, go ahead and pitch," he said, kicking the grass in frustration. "But next inning, it's one of us."

Haley rolled the first ball to Matt Braddock, who kicked it so hard it shot like a bullet across the field and out into the street. Instantly Shannon and the other sitters leapt to their feet.

"Stop at the curb and look both ways," Shannon cautioned Suzi Barrett, who was running after the ball. "There are cars coming."

Suzi looked left and then right. And left and then right again. In the meantime, Matt Braddock had rounded second base and was heading for third.

"Get the ball!" Jordan screamed. "Suzi! Go get the ball."

"Okay, Suzi," Shannon called after a car had driven past. "It's all clear."

Suzi raced across the street just as Matt

crossed home plate. Buddy jumped in the air and gave him a high-five. "Score one for us!" Buddy shouted.

"That's not fair!" Margo, who was playing second base, pouted. "There was a car coming and Suzi couldn't get the ball."

"Yeah," Jordan agreed. "That probably should have been called a foul ball. Or we should have stopped the game."

"You're just saying that because we scored a run," Buddy replied.

"You guys sound like a bunch of babies," Nicky added as he waited in line behind Buddy. "If you didn't have such a bad pitcher, that wouldn't have happened."

Haley glared at Nicky. Then she rolled the ball as hard as she could, and it bounced up and hit him square in the chest.

"Ow!" Nicky yelped.

"Uh-oh," Stacey said. "Now they're getting mean. Maybe we should say something."

Mal grabbed Stacey's arm. "The triplets said they could handle it. Let's see what they do."

They did nothing. Adam, Byron, and Jordan stood by helplessly while Nicky raced to retrieve the ball, then heaved it back at Haley. Haley ducked and the ball bounced off Margo, who kicked it back at Nicky as hard as she could. The ball sailed over the big rock at the edge of Brenner Field and disappeared.

"That's great," Nicky yelled. "Now you've lost our ball."

"I didn't lose it," Margo replied. "I returned it to you."

"Go get it," Nicky ordered.

"No! You get it."

Luckily for them, Norman Hill stuck his head around the side of the rock. "Are you guys looking for this?"

"Throw it to me, Norman!" Haley ordered. "I'm the pitcher."

Norman held onto the ball. "Can I play?"

"Sure," said Becca Ramsey. "You can be on our team."

"No, he can't," Jordan protested. "That would give you one more guy than us. Besides, the game's already started."

"It's hardly started at all," Byron shot back. "I say he can play."

"Oh, great!" Mallory rolled her eyes. "Now the captains are fighting."

"If you ask me," Claud remarked as she passed around a bag of chocolate stars, "I don't think this kickball team has much hope of making it to the end of the game."

"I don't think they'll make it to the next out," Stacey said as they watched Byron and Jordan scream at each other.

"I really think we should help them," Shannon said. "This kickball team is a wonderful idea."

"Shannon's right," Jessi agreed. "It's a great activity for the neighborhood. Ever since the team was formed, Becca has hardly talked about anything else."

Mallory chewed anxiously on the edge of one nail. "I know the team is important, but I promised the triplets I wouldn't interfere."

"Just pitch the ball!" Buddy hollered. He was standing at the plate, anxious to kick a home run.

"Not if Norman is going to be on your team," Haley replied. "You have too many players."

"One more kid won't matter," Margo said.

"Let's just *play*, okay?" Suzi pleaded.

"Haley, pitch the ball!" the other players on her team shouted.

"No!" Haley stuck out her tongue at them.

"I'll pitch the ball," Adam said, stepping up to the pitchers' mound. "Here, let me have it."

"No!" Haley clutched the ball to her stomach and fell to her knees. "I'm the pitcher."

"Well, a pitcher pitches," Adam said, trying to pry her fingers off the ball.

"Ow!" Haley cried out. "You're breaking my knuckles."

"Then let go!"

"Leave her alone!" Margo dove between Adam and Haley.

Jordan stood in centerfield and screamed at the top of his lungs, "Will *someone* please pitch the ball?"

Matt signed to Nicky and Nicky said, "Matt says he's got another ball. He'll go home to get it."

Claud leapt to her feet. "Uh-oh. Haley's not going to be happy when she sees Matt with a different ball."

Mallory raised one eyebrow. "Claud . . ."

"I know, I know." Claudia flopped onto the grass again. "Let the triplets handle it. It's their team."

Stacey leaned back on her elbows in the grass. "This should be really interesting. Two balls in one game."

Matt bolted for home and returned a little while later, holding a brown ball over his head in triumph. Adam saw the ball and let go of Haley.

"Okay, Matt," Adam said, waving his hands in the air. "I'm the pitcher now. Throw it to me."

Matt tossed the ball and Adam stepped in front of Haley, who was still curled up in the dirt clutching the other ball.

Buddy waited at the plate. But before Adam

could throw the ball, Margo shouted, "You throw that ball, Adam Pike, and I quit!"

Jordan looked as if he were about to cry. His team was falling apart. Best friends were shouting at each other, brothers and sisters were fighting. Nothing was going the way he'd planned. But he didn't ask for help from anyone. Instead he said, "This game is canceled. Due to rain."

Then Adam, Jordan, and Byron stalked off the field. The remaining kids looked stunned. They stood silently for a long time, hoping the triplets would return.

Finally Mal stood up. "You heard the team captains," she announced to the group. "The game has been canceled."

"But I still want to play," Suzi said, crossing to Shannon. "Why can't we play?"

Shannon shrugged. "Because everyone was fighting too much. We need to be getting back, anyway. Your mother should be home from her meeting any time now."

"Boy," Buddy grumbled as Shannon walked Suzi and Buddy home. "That was the stupidest game I've ever played."

"I don't think the game's the problem," Shannon said carefully. "The team just needs to make some rules and stick with them."

"Well, if the next game is as awful as this," Buddy declared, "I don't want to play."

Shannon didn't say anything. All the way back to the Barrett house, she wondered whether she and the other BSC members had done the right thing by not interfering. As things stood now the future of the kickball team looked pretty grim.

# CHAPTER 10

$D$*ing-dong.*

I rang the bell at the Prezziosos' house on Wednesday afternoon, and waited for Jenny's usual round of questions. But she didn't even say, "Who is it?" Instead the door just flew open.

"Come on in," Jenny called over her shoulder as she marched back into the living room. "Mom and the *star* are getting their coats."

The star? Jenny had never called Andrea that before.

"Does Andrea have a callback today?" I asked.

"No, she has a job," Jenny said, flopping on the couch in the living room. "I didn't even get an audition. Nobody wants to see me."

I have to admit, I was paying a little more attention to what Jenny was doing than what she was saying. Or what she *wasn't* doing. She wasn't sitting stiffly on a wooden chair, making sure she didn't wrinkle her dress or tights. She was slumped down on the couch, her dress bunched up behind her and a big smudge on the knee of her tights. What was going on?

Mrs. Prezzioso stuck her head into the room. "Hello, Mary Anne. I'm sorry we can't chat, but Andrea has to meet with the wardrobe people in twenty minutes."

"Good for Andrea," Jenny muttered.

Mrs. Prezzioso didn't seem to hear her. She just smiled pleasantly and said, "The studio number is on the refrigerator. Take care. Good-bye, my angel."

Jenny didn't even look at her mother. She waited until she heard the front door close and then said, "I'm thirsty. Let's have juice."

"Okay." I followed her into the kitchen. "Do you want me to pour?"

"No, I can do it." Jenny got a pitcher of cranapple juice from the refrigerator while I found two glasses and some napkins. She started pouring the instant I'd set the glass down. In fact, she poured the first one so full it overflowed onto the kitchen counter. It also splattered down the front of her white pinafore but Jenny didn't seem to notice. Amazing!

"Here, Jenny," I said, grabbing a sponge and dabbing at her dress and the counter. "Why don't you let me pour the next glass?"

"I can do it!" Jenny jerked the pitcher out of my reach, splashing more juice on her dress. Some landed on her tights this time, too. Again, she didn't seem to care.

I held my glass as she poured, and stopped her before she could overfill it.

Jenny held up her glass. "First one finished, wins." Then she tilted her head back and drank the entire glass straight down. She slammed the glass on the counter. "Ahhh!"

Now Jenny not only had juice on her tights, on her sleeve, and down the front of her pinafore, she had a big red juice moustache on her upper lip, too. I handed her a napkin, expecting to see her dab at her mouth politely, but she just gave her face a swipe, bunched the napkin into a wad and tossed it on the table. "Let's go outside and play."

Jenny was moving so fast I could hardly keep up with her. "Don't you want to change into your playclothes?" I asked, picking up the napkin and throwing it in the trash.

"No. These clothes are fine." Jenny bolted out the back door and headed for the sandbox. Actually, that afternoon it was more of a mud-puddle pit. It had rained the night before and the wooden box was filled with murky brown water.

Last week's Miss Priss wouldn't have gone within twenty feet of it. But Jenny-the-Slob

93

splashed right in. Specks of brown dotted her face. Her shiny black patent leather shoes disappeared beneath the pool of water and her tights were stained a yucky brown color up to her knees.

"I'm going to make a mud pie," Jenny said, grinning at me from behind her mud speckles and red moustache. "For Andrea."

"Well, that's very thoughtful of you," I replied. At least she was smiling. And she hadn't been near the sink yet. Whatever was going on, she certainly seemed to be over her cleanliness obsession.

Jenny scooped up big handfuls of drippy sand and leaves and patted it all together. "I'll put in some sticks and rocks, and maybe even a few worms," she declared. "Then she can eat them for dinner."

"Worms?" I wrinkled my nose. "Nobody likes to eat worms."

"*Andrea* will eat *anything*," Jenny said in a sing-song voice. "Andrea will *do* anything. She's the perfect baby."

I knelt beside the sandbox. (I'd managed to find a dry patch.) "Jenny, Andrea's not perfect," I said. "Nobody's perfect."

"She is too!" Jenny stuck out her lower lip. "Everybody loves Andrea. She gets all the jobs."

Now the picture was becoming clearer. Jenny's career as a model and child actress wasn't going well. Andrea's was. Jenny was doubly jealous.

"Of course Andrea gets more jobs than you. There are more jobs for baby models."

Jenny paused with her sand shovel in the air. "There are?"

I don't know much about the acting business, but I did remember the things Mrs. Prezzioso had told me. "Sure. Think of all the extra things babies use. Diapers, talcum powder, diaper rash ointment, baby wipes, baby food, baby clothes, baby walkers, baby strollers, baby car seats, baby cribs."

Jenny narrowed her eyes at me, checking to see if I was telling the truth. So I went on. "But the biggest reason Andrea is getting more work is that babies don't have to act. Andrea just has to be a baby. You have to be a model *and* an actress."

Jenny tapped her cheek with the shovel and thought out loud. "Andrea just has to smile. I have to walk and say stuff. And cry."

"That's right. You really have to act."

"But I haven't gotten a job." Jenny scooped her shovel back into the water and flung mud at the pie. "That must mean I'm a bad actress."

Oh, brother. I thought I was making things better. I'd only made them worse.

Suddenly the air was filled with the sound

of jack-in-the-box music. I hummed along with the familiar tune before I remembered the words. "Pop goes the weasel. Someone is playing that song," I said.

Jenny perked up. "It's the ice cream man!"

"Would you like an ice cream?" I asked her.

"Okay." Jenny dropped her shovel and stepped out of the sandbox. She looked like Pig-Pen from the Peanuts comic strip. "Come on, let's go."

I hesitated for only a second. If she didn't mind her appearance, I guessed I didn't, either. We followed the music and caught up with the ice cream truck on Slate Street.

The driver, an older gentleman with a gray moustache and round glasses, took one look at Jenny and said, "Young lady! What happened? Did you have an accident?"

Jenny glanced down at her mud-soaked tights and red-and-brown splotched dress. "No," she replied. "I was just playing."

She chose a pink and orange swirlsicle and it got good and drippy before she was finished. The parts of her face and dress that weren't already decorated with mud or cran-apple juice were now streaked with sticky pink and orange Popsicle juice. She was a mess.

"My!" The ice cream man chuckled. "You've certainly given that pretty dress a new look. How do you think your mother will like it?"

Jenny shrugged. "She'll probably be mad."

But Jenny didn't seem the least bit upset. As I thought about that, a light clicked on in my brain. Now I understood why Miss Priss had become Miss Mess. She wanted her mom to notice her. If she couldn't get her mother's attention by being the perfect child, she was sure to get it by being the perfect slob.

I realized something else, too. "Your mother won't be mad at *you*," I said, taking Jenny by one of her sticky hands and leading her across the street. "She'll be mad at me for letting you get this way."

"Where are we going?" Jenny asked.

"Home," I replied. "We have just enough time to get you out of that dress and into a bath."

"No." Jenny locked her knees and wouldn't budge. "I don't want a bath."

I envisioned Mrs. Prezzioso coming home and finding Jenny sitting in the living room, looking as if she'd spent the afternoon playing at the garbage dump. I had no idea what Mrs. P. would do or say but I knew she wouldn't be happy.

"Look, Jenny, I am responsible for you and your clothes," I said firmly. "You need a bath, and that dress needs to soak in soapy water, too — *before* your mom comes home."

Jenny gave in and I managed to clean her

up before Mrs. Prezzioso and Andrea returned. But I was worried about Jenny again. So worried that I called Dawn that evening to see if she could offer any advice.

It was three hours earlier in California, of course. Dawn had just gotten home from school. "Schafer residence. This is Dawn."

She sounded as if she were just down the street and I remembered what it used to be like, before she left for California, before our parents got married, and before we moved into the same house and became stepsisters, when we were just best friends.

"Hi, it's me," I said.

I held the phone away from my ear as Dawn shrieked, "I was just thinking about you! I swear. On the way home from school, I saw this gray-striped kitten that looked just like Tigger, and I thought about when you first got Tigger, and when he moved into our house on Burnt Hill Road. Remember? He mewed all the time and nearly drove Mom and me crazy!"

I giggled thinking about it. "Well, he's completely at home here now," I said. "He spends his time lounging around the house, acting as if he owns the place."

"I miss Tigger," Dawn said, wistfully. "And I miss you."

"I miss you, too." I could feel a lump forming in my throat (I told you I cry at the least little thing). "I really wish you were here now. I need some help with Jenny."

"Miss Priss?" Dawn asked. I'd told her about Jenny the last time we'd talked, a couple of weeks earlier. But Dawn didn't know things had changed in a *big* way.

"Now she's become Miss Mess," I said.

"Miss Mess? That's hard to believe. How?"

It took almost fifteen minutes (which is my absolute limit on long distance phone calls) for me to describe Jenny's transformation from the neatest, primmest little girl in Stoneybrook to the neighborhood slob — and why it had happened.

"What should I do about it?" I asked.

"I'm not sure if you *can* do anything," Dawn said, "except let Jenny know you like her even though she isn't a super model."

"I'm trying to do that."

"Have you talked to the BSC about this?"

"Not about the new Miss Mess. I thought I'd talk it over with you first."

"Well, I'd bring it up on Friday," Dawn suggested. "Think of all the other problems we've solved at meetings."

Dawn was right. It was time for some BSC brainstorming.

## CHAPTER 11

"We'll skip the announcements and get right down to business," Kristy said, the moment Claud's digital clock turned from five-twenty-nine to five-thirty. "Mary Anne is worried about Jenny Prezzioso and needs our advice. So I'm giving the floor to Mary Anne."

When I had called Kristy earlier to see if we could set aside some time during the meeting to talk about Jenny, Kristy had said pretty much what Dawn had said. "That's what we're here for."

So I reviewed the events of the past few weeks and then told everybody what had happened the day before. "Now Jenny has turned into Pig-Pen," I finished up. "I'm not kidding. She's a complete mess."

Kristy leaned forward in the director's chair. "So you think this started because Jenny felt Mrs. Prezzioso had abandoned her? I mean, Mrs. P. has been gone an awful lot, right?"

I nodded. "Every afternoon and quite a few mornings. She takes Andrea and leaves Jenny behind."

Jessi shrugged. "I'd probably feel just like Jenny. Left out."

"First she tried getting her mom's attention by being perfect, because she thinks Andrea is perfect," I said. "She's been hearing people rave about Andrea constantly."

"Andrea *is* a pretty wonderful baby," Stacey said. "She hardly ever cries. She goes to sleep when you put her in her crib and when she's awake, she smiles all the time like a perfect angel." Stacey covered her mouth when she realized what she'd said. "Oops."

"That's okay," I reassured her. "It's easy to say that. But Andrea is just a baby. I'm sure things will change as she gets older and learns to say words like no and why. Right now, though, she really is getting all the attention — and all the jobs. I think that's why Jenny turned into Miss Mess. Andrea is a big success and Jenny can't even get one commercial. She thinks she's a flop at age four."

"Right," Kristy said. "She feels awful. And now she wants to see if being a mess will make her parents notice her."

"It's hard *not* to notice her." I laughed. "Yesterday she was covered from head to toe in mud, cranapple juice, and Popsicle goo."

"Don't the Prezziosos see what's going on?" Stacey asked.

I shook my head. "I don't think so. Yesterday Mrs. Prezzioso acted like everything was perfectly normal. Of course, she didn't see Jenny's redesigned dress. But it isn't just Jenny's clothes, it's the way she's acting."

Claudia sighed. "Mary Anne, I think you better talk to Mrs. Prezzioso. If you don't, who knows what Jenny will do next?"

"I agree with Claud," Kristy said. "But how do you tell someone their kid is in trouble and it's kind of their fault?"

"Be careful what you say," Shannon warned me. "If the Prezziosos think you're blaming them for Jenny's behavior, they might get really upset."

"And we don't want to get a reputation for being too pushy," Kristy added. "That could hurt the club."

"Well, no one could ever accuse us of being pushy with the Pike kids," Stacey said, moving on to another subject. "We've been completely hands-off."

"Even with all the arguing at that last kickball game. It was a disaster," Shannon said, rolling her eyes. "I think we could have intervened at least ten times, but we didn't."

Claudia laughed. "That took a *lot* of willpower."

"The triplets are trying to prove they don't need a baby-sitter," I said. "But I'm not sure."

Kristy adjusted her visor. "I think the triplets are right. They probably are too old for a baby-sitter."

"But they're not old enough to *be* baby-sitters," Jessi pointed out.

"You can say that again," Shannon said. "They don't know how to handle kids. They boss their friends around without thinking about anybody's feelings."

"But then, when they *should* be bossy," Claudia added, "like during some of those fights last week, they wimp out."

"Well, something has to be done about them." Shannon folded her arms across her chest. "Otherwise the kickball team will just collapse."

"Half of the kids have already threatened to quit," Jessi added. "Becca included."

"I think we should call Mallory," Kristy said, picking up the phone. "Maybe she has a solution."

"I hope she's home," Claud said.

"I'm sure she's home," Jessi replied. "Her parents still won't let her go anywhere after school."

Jessi was right. Mallory was home. And not only was she home, she was baby-sitting. Again.

"Mom asked me to look after Vanessa, Margo, and Claire while she took the boys for their yearly check-up," Mallory explained. "So once more I'm stuck sitting at home. I should change my title from the Pikes' daughter to the Pikes' nanny."

Kristy got right to the point. "Mal, we're worried about the triplets and the kickball team."

"Me too," Mallory replied. "My brothers have a great idea but I'm afraid they're going to blow it."

"Is there any way you could talk to them?" Kristy asked. "I mean, just to give them some friendly advice?"

"It's funny you should mention it," Mal said. "I've been making a list of suggestions to give them about how to organize a team. And deal with the problems that come up."

"Do you think they'll read it?"

"If I present it to them right. I thought I'd tell them about the BSC, and how it was first formed. I'll make a point of bringing up some of the problems we've faced with each other and our clients and how we went about solving them. Then I'll ask if they've run into any troubles like that with their team."

"Great," Kristy said, with an approving nod. "Be sure and compliment them on what a good idea it was to form a neighborhood kickball team."

"Don't worry, I will. I'll talk to them tomorrow afternoon, when Mom takes Vanessa and Margo to the dentist."

"You're baby-sitting again tomorrow?"

"I'm *always* baby-sitting," Mallory grumbled. "Since my parents won't let me do anything else, I'm always available."

"That's terrible," Kristy murmured sympathetically.

"It's weird, but I was looking at my calendar yesterday and I realized that I'm baby-sitting more now than before I got sick."

"Do your parents know that?" Kristy asked.

"They should. They're the ones who are hiring me."

"Mal, I think it's time for you to talk to your parents."

Mallory heaved a huge sigh. "I tell them I'm well but they don't believe me."

"Don't talk about being well or sick," Kristy suggested. "Talk about being overbooked. Show them your sitting schedule. Draw a chart."

"They'd probably be shocked."

"They should be," Kristy said indignantly. "Then after you've shown them your chart, tell them you have to rejoin the BSC."

"I wish," Mallory murmured. "I sure miss you guys."

"We miss you, too," Kristy said, her voice softening. "It's time you came home."

The rest of us, who had been listening to Kristy's side of the phone conversation, nodded to each other.

"Come back, Mallory!" Claudia shouted.

"We need you," Stacey called.

"We miss you," Jessi and I added.

"Tell everybody thanks," Mallory said to Kristy. "And tell them I'm going to talk to my parents. I just need to come up with a surefire plan of attack."

After Kristy had hung up, she filled us in on her discussion with Mallory. Hearing that Mallory had decided to talk to the triplets *and* her parents gave my courage a boost.

"I *am* going to talk to Mrs. Prezzioso," I said suddenly.

"When?" Claud asked.

I took a deep breath. "Tomorrow. I'll talk to her tomorrow."

"What are you going to say?" Kristy asked.

"I'm not sure," I replied. "I'll have to think about that."

# CHAPTER 12

I had huge butterflies in my stomach all day Thursday. In my head, I rehearsed what I might say to Mrs. Prezzioso. I knew the direct approach was always best but I didn't want to be too pushy. Once I decided what I would say to Mrs. Prezzioso, I was faced with another problem. When would I tell her? Before or after my sitting job?

Mrs. Prezzioso was standing on the front porch looking very anxious when I arrived that afternoon. For half a second I thought I was late.

"Mary Anne, I'm so glad you're early," Mrs. Prezzioso said. "The agency just called and, if I hurry, I can squeeze in two auditions this afternoon."

Now was definitely not a good time to have a heart-to-heart. I waved good-bye to her, and decided that later was the better choice anyway. The audition would be over and she would be more relaxed. Maybe I would be, too.

Boy, was I wrong. Looking after Jenny that day was anything but relaxing. All afternoon she went from room to room, making one mess after another.

The living room was her first target. I found her sitting in the center of the rug with a big mound of Clay-Mate in front of her.

"Jenny!" I gasped. "What are you doing?"

"Making cookies. What's it look like?"

"It looks like a mess." Hurriedly, I started peeling the clay off the rug. "You have to play with this on the kitchen table, Jenny. You know that."

"I think it's more fun on the floor." Jenny picked up an oatmeal box — the round kind — she'd brought in from the kitchen and started to use it like a rolling pin, trying to flatten out the remaining clay. Unfortunately the lid wasn't on tight.

"Jenny! Look out. There's oatmeal pouring out of the box." I grabbed the box before she could do any more damage. But the clay was already covered with pale white oat flakes. "Okay. Clay time is over. Why don't you put the clay back in the container while I vacuum?"

Jenny reluctantly scooped the clay into its bucket. I ran the vacuum, and then picked the last bits of clay out of the rug by hand.

"There!" I said when I was done. "You can barely tell anything happened." But I was talking to myself.

While I was cleaning, Jenny had wandered upstairs to her room. When I caught up with her, she was setting up a little easel by her bed. "I want to paint," she said.

I knew that her mother kept the easel in the closet, along with a big plastic apron for Jenny and a plastic cloth for the floor. Jenny had ignored both of them. Before I could stop her, she opened a jar of red paint and promptly dropped it on the parquet floor.

"Don't move an inch," I ordered. "I'll get a cloth to clean that up."

At least she missed the rug, I thought as I raced down to the kitchen. I grabbed a sponge, a roll of paper towels, and some spray cleaner, and tossed the things in the pink plastic bucket under the sink. I had a feeling that this was going to be a very messy afternoon, and I'd better be prepared.

"Jenny, let's pretend we're Cinderella and her fairy godmother and we have to make sure this floor is sparkling clean if we want to go to the ball. I'll wipe up the big globs of paint and you can sponge up the rest."

Jenny took the sponge but made only a couple of half-hearted swipes at the floor. She wasn't terribly interested in pretending to be Cinderella, and she definitely didn't want to make anything look clean.

After I'd washed out the sponge and thrown away the paper towels, I laid the plastic mat under the easel. "Shall we work on your painting now?"

Jenny made a face. "Nope. I'm done with painting." She skipped out of the room.

"Wait for me," I called as I folded up the easel and put away the drop cloth. I grabbed my bucket and hurried after Jenny. She'd been out of my sight for two minutes. Plenty of time to get into more trouble. Messy trouble.

I found Jenny in the front entryway with a broom and a golf ball. She was trying to tap the golf ball into one of her father's shoes. "Is this putting practice?" I asked.

She nodded seriously, eyeing her target. "Daddy does it all the time."

Actually, Jenny's golf stance, complete with broom and golf ball, made a cute picture. I was just starting to think that Miss Mess might actually be an improvement over Miss Priss, when she hauled off and swung the broom like a professional golfer. The broom clipped the vase of lilacs perched on the side table, and water and flowers flew everywhere.

"Oh, no!" I gasped. I leapt forward and managed to catch the vase before it could hit the floor and break into a thousand pieces.

Even Jenny looked mortified. She dropped the broom and turned pale. But once she realized that the vase hadn't broken she left.

I couldn't believe the way she was behaving. "Jenny! Would you please come back here?"

"Why?" she called from the kitchen.

"Because you knocked over these flowers and you need to pick them up. I've got paper towels and a sponge for the water, but I'm going to need help with the lilacs."

"Oh, all right." She stomped into the entryway and scooped the flowers into a clump on the floor. "There."

"Nope." I shook my head. "In the vase."

Jenny dropped the flowers in the vase one by one, as if she were dropping stones into a bucket. When she was finished I said, "Thank you, Jenny. You were a very good helper."

"I want to go outside." Jenny walked to the back door without giving me another look.

It hadn't rained for a couple of days but I imagined the sandbox was still pretty soggy. The thought of Jenny covered in mud again made me race to head her off at the pass.

"Hold it. Hold it," I said, blocking the back door. "I'd love to go outside, too, but why don't we go to the playground? Maybe some other kids will be there and you could swing."

I thought a walk to Stoneybrook Elementary's playground would be a safe way to keep Jenny clean. Wrong!

There must have been ten big puddles between her house and the school yard and Jenny sloshed through every one of them. Then she picked up a kickball lying at the edge of the playground and hugged it to her chest, smearing the front of her dress with dirt.

I sighed. "Jenny, why don't we do a little kickball practice," I suggested, eyeing the playing field. Since she was already dirty, we might as well have some fun.

Jenny brightened. "Okay. You be the pitcher," she said, tossing me the ball. "I'll kick."

I rolled the ball toward her. Jenny wound up and kicked the ball with all her might. Unfortunately, she missed the ball completely, and the force of her kick sent her sprawling backward onto the grass. Now she had a bright green grass stain on the back of her skirt.

"Are you okay?" I asked, rushing to help her stand.

Jenny held out her left wrist and winced. "I think I hurt my hand. Maybe I need a Band-Aid."

I saw a few scrapes on her palm, but I was more concerned about bits of gravel and grass getting into them. "I don't know if you need a Band-Aid, but we should wash this. We wouldn't want it to get infected."

Back we went to her house. This time Jenny avoided the puddles. I think she was too busy worrying about her hand.

"Jenny, why don't you wait in the kitchen while I get the first aid kit from upstairs?"

"Okay."

I trudged up the stairs to the linen closet where the Prezziosos stored their first aid kit. Normally I would have thought the afternoon's events were funny, but not today. In the first place, every mess Jenny made, I had to clean up. And in the second place, I was still worrying about what I was going to say to Mrs. Prezzioso.

The only good thing about the afternoon was that it was almost over. I checked the clock in the upstairs hall. Mrs. Prezzioso was due home in ten minutes. That gave me just enough time to wash Jenny's wound and wipe the worst of the mud stains off the front of her dress.

I carried the Band-Aids, hydrogen peroxide, and some cotton balls into the kitchen. But when I arrived, it looked as though a tornado had struck. A peanut butter tornado.

In the short time I'd been gone, Jenny had gotten a jar of peanut butter out of the cupboard, opened it, and started to make a sandwich. There was peanut butter everywhere. I'm not kidding. It was smeared on the counter and down the front of the refrigerator. The silverware drawer was open, and its handle was coated with the stuff. A trail of peanut butter globs led toward the dining room.

"Jenny Prezzioso!" I shouted. "You come in here this instant. I mean it. This instant."

I don't lose my temper very often. But Jenny and the peanut butter had pushed things over the top.

Jenny, hearing the anger in my voice, stuck her head timidly into the room. Her cheeks were smeared with peanut butter. I could guess what her dress and hands looked like.

"Oops," was all she said.

"Oops?" I looked at the clock. There was barely enough time to clean the peanut butter off the floor. I had no idea how Mrs. Prezzioso was going to react to this mess. I felt terrible.

"Oh, Jenny." I slumped down in the chair by the kitchen table and sighed. "This is a big problem. A really big problem."

Naturally the door opened at that moment. "Hello, you two," Mrs. Prezzioso called. "We're home."

This was it. I was probably going to get fired. Maybe Mrs. Prezzioso would fire the whole BSC. "We're in the kitchen," I called meekly. "And we've had kind of an accident."

"An accident? What do you . . . ?" Mrs. Prezzioso stopped in her tracks when she saw the kitchen.

"I'm so sorry," I said. "This happened a few minutes ago when I was upstairs getting a Band-Aid. I just haven't had a chance to clean it up yet."

"Don't worry, Mary Anne." Mrs. Prezzioso set Andrea in her high chair and got a cracker from the cupboard. "I'm not upset with you. Or this mess."

"You're not?"

Mrs. Prezzioso turned to face her peanut butter-covered daughter. I was certain she was going to blow up at her but instead she said, "Jenny, my angel, will you help Mommy and Mary Anne clean up?"

"Okay," said Jenny.

"Well, first, why don't you change out of that dress and put it in the hamper. And then you can find some play clothes to put on."

When she was safely upstairs and out of hearing, Mrs. Prezzioso turned to me and sighed. "She's really become a problem, Mary Anne. Mr. Prezzioso and I know that she's jealous of Andrea and just acting out her feelings, but we're not sure what to do about it."

Boy, was I relieved. All of my butterflies disappeared and I was able to talk easily. "I know she's competing with Andrea," I said as

115

I cleaned off the kitchen counter. "First she tried being perfect."

"Then she wanted to be an actress," Mrs. Prezzioso said, picking up a sponge and helping me. "But Andrea is doing so well, Jenny can't possibly compete."

"So now she's making messes." I tackled the silverware drawer. "This one was her best yet."

Mrs. Prezzioso shuddered. "I think I've picked up her room three times today. And her clothes get dirty the instant she puts them on."

"It's hard to keep her away from mud puddles," I added. "And out of that wet sandbox."

Mrs. Prezzioso leaned against the refrigerator. "I wish I knew what to do."

"Maybe Jenny's upset because you're spending so much more time with Andrea," I said hesitantly.

"I know, but that's because Andrea has so many jobs and auditions." Mrs. Prezzioso folded her dishtowel neatly and placed it on the counter. "I suppose Andrea could stop doing commercials, but that money is going to guarantee her an education."

"You can still find ways to spend extra time with Jenny," I suggested. "Just the two of you.

I could sit for Andrea while you take Jenny shopping, or out for a soda."

"That sounds wonderful, but it won't be easy to find time. Andrea and I are gone nearly every afternoon."

I didn't have an answer to that one. "Well, maybe Jenny will get a job soon," I said doubtfully.

"Maybe." Mrs. Prezzioso sounded just as doubtful. "I know that would make her feel better."

"Mommy!" Jenny called from the top of the stairs. "Can you help me pick out an outfit? I can't make up my mind."

Mrs. Prezzioso looked at me and then at the clock. "Mary Anne, do you mind . . . ?"

My job was officially over but I wanted to let the two of them have a little time alone together. Even if it was only for ten minutes.

"Go ahead," I said. "I'll keep an eye on Andrea."

"Thanks." Mrs. Prezzioso gave my shoulder a squeeze as she left the kitchen. While she and Jenny were upstairs, I finished cleaning up the peanut butter. Mrs. Prezzioso had been very understanding, but I know it's best if a baby-sitter leaves a house in the same condition she found it.

When I walked home that afternoon I felt

encouraged. And discouraged, too. Jenny's problem was finally out in the open and I knew her parents were taking it seriously, but nobody had found a solution. That meant Jenny was still unhappy. She could change again. But how? She'd already been Miss Priss and Miss Mess. What next? I hated to imagine it.

Saturday

Siting for the Pikes is hard werk! I know ther are only seven of you, mal, but today it felt like seventy.

Claud's right. It was a disaster day at my house. Every kid in my family had an accident of some kind.

mal and I woud just clean up one spill when Nicky or Claire wood spill sumthing else.

And the triplets—

That's a whole OTHER starry...

119

I'm glad I wasn't at the Pikes' that Saturday. Cleaning up after Jenny's messes was hard enough. I hated to think about cleaning up after seven kids!

The disasters started before Claudia even walked through the door. Nicky met her on his bike in the driveway.

"Claudia, look — no hands!" Nicky waved his arms in the air. He was so busy trying to get her attention that he didn't notice the wagon full of toys blocking the sidewalk.

"Nicky, look out!" Claudia cried, but it was too late.

*Crash!* The bike hit the wagon and toys flew everywhere. Luckily Nicky was tossed onto the grass. Still, he hit the ground with a heavy thump.

"Owwwwwww!" he moaned.

Claudia ran to him.

"Are you okay, Nicky?" she asked as she knelt beside him.

He didn't answer right away but lay spread-eagled on the ground, staring up at the sky. "Did I break my bike?" he asked.

Claud glanced at the bike, which lay under the wagon. "I think the front fender's bent."

"Oh, I bent that last week."

"And one of the tires looks low."

"It's always low."

Claud shrugged. "Then I guess the bike's okay. But how are *you* doing?"

"My elbows hurt." Nicky sat up slowly, bending his arms to check the damage. His elbows were matted with bits of grass and dirt and one was a little bloody.

Claudia winced. "That scrape looks like it hurts. I better get you inside so we can wash that and fix it up."

She helped Nicky to his feet and into the house.

"Get on board! Get on board," Claire called as they made their way into the kitchen. She was sitting in a yellow cardboard box in the center of the room. "I'm the Magic School Bus."

"Hello, Magic School Bus," Claud said. "Will you give me a ride?"

"Sure. Hop in." Claire scooted the box forward just as Vanessa entered the room carrying two milk carton planters filled with marigolds that she was growing for a school project.

"Ouch!" Vanessa yelped as Claire's box rammed her in the shins. The milk cartons flew out of her hands and potting soil and flowers exploded everywhere.

Dirt showered on Claire's head. "Ew! Get it off!"

"My project!" Vanessa wailed. "Claire wrecked it!"

Claudia, who was trying to tend Nicky's elbow, yelled, "Mallory! Are you in the house?"

"Yes," Mal called from upstairs. "I'm just cleaning up the bathroom."

"I need your help in the kitchen. We've had a collision."

Mal hurried down the stairs. She was carrying two mops and a bucket of sponges. "We just had a flood in the bathroom. Margo thought it would be a good idea to give Pow a bath, so she started the water running and forgot about it."

"Claire ruined my science project," Vanessa whined.

"You know that was an accident," Claudia said as she carefully cleaned Nicky's arm with a wet washcloth. "If you'll just be patient, Mal and I will help you with it."

Mal dropped to her knees and helped Vanessa scoop dirt back into the milk cartons. "It's like a three-ring circus today," Mal said.

She had just finished mopping the dirt off the floor when Claire stepped out of her yellow school bus. "I feel icky." She bent over from the waist and shook her head like a dog. Dirt sprayed everywhere.

"More dirt!" Claud exclaimed.

"All over the clean floor," Mallory moaned.

*Wham!*

The back screen door sounded as though it had been torn off its hinges. Adam stormed into the kitchen.

"Don't step in the — " Adam stomped in the middle of Claire's mess and glared at Mallory. "Dirt," Claudia finished meekly.

"I give up." Mallory slid to the floor. She let go of her mops and they clattered down beside her.

"Where is everybody?" Adam demanded.

Mal and Claud looked at each other and Claud replied, "Well, Claire is right there with the yellow box. Your sister, Vanessa, is over by the sink, watering her marigolds. Nicky, as you can see, is inspecting his crash wounds at the kitchen table — "

"And Margo is watching TV," Mal finished. "Does that answer your question?"

The screen door slammed again and Byron and Jordan appeared. "Still no sign of anybody," Byron reported.

"We scheduled a kickball game today but nobody showed up," Adam explained to Mal and Claud.

"Not even our own brothers and sisters," Jordan said, scowling at Claire and Nicky.

Nicky looked up from examining his elbow. "Well, if you were better captains,

123

maybe kids would come back."

"What do you mean?" Adam asked.

"You can never make up your minds."

"All anybody ever does during the kickball game is fight," Margo added, joining the kids in the kitchen.

"Well, what do you want us to do?" Adam said. "Yell at people? Put them in time out?"

Mallory cleared her throat. This was the moment she was waiting for. "Adam, I know how you feel about baby-sitters interfering, but I think Claud and I could offer you some ideas about handling kids."

Claudia nodded. "In the BSC we always share baby-sitting tips."

Adam folded his arms across his chest. "Look, we can be just as good as you guys."

Mallory smiled. "Of course you can. But it takes a little practice." She stood up and moved into the dining room, where she'd stashed her sheet of suggestions. "I made a list of a few good ways to handle problems. Can I share it with you?"

Byron and Jordan shrugged.

"Sure," Adam said. "But we don't need you telling us what to do."

"I'm not going to." Mallory set the list on the dining room table. "But I do think you need to make some decisions before you get together with the kids again. Like how you're going to run your team."

"But everyone *else* is trying to run it," Byron said. "As soon as we get together they start fighting."

"That's why it's important to establish the ground rules," Claudia said. "For instance, you guys might decide that anyone who wants to play can be on the team. That's a ground rule. That means that there won't be any arguing about who can or can't play."

Jordan looked at Byron. "That makes sense."

"Sure," Mallory said. "And if you make a rule that everyone can be allowed to pitch, then you set up a system for picking the order. You can draw straws or go alphabetically. You choose a system, and stick with it."

Adam smiled. "I like that."

"But what if kids start shouting at each other?" Byron asked.

Claudia shrugged. "You let them know that fighting will not be allowed on the field. If they fight, they're automatically suspended for the rest of the game."

"They might have some real complaints, though," Mallory said. "So it's important to allow time after the game or once a week for people to tell you their problems. That's something we always do at BSC meetings."

"Being a baby-sitter or team captain is a lot like being a diplomat," Claudia said with a smile. "You have to be nice but firm."

The triplets seemed excited. After a long discussion, they put together a good list of rules.

"This is great," Adam said afterwards. "I want to go talk to the kids right now."

"Be back by dinner," Mal started to call after the triplets but she clapped her hand over her mouth. Then she said, "I mean, Mom and Dad said they'd be home around five-thirty. Would you guys make sure that Nicky, Margo, and Claire don't run off?"

"Sure, we'll take good care of them," Adam said, pausing in the doorway of the dining room. "Oh, and uh, thanks for the advice."

Claudia grinned at Mallory after the boys had left. "You handled that really well. I think the kickball team has a chance now."

Mallory smiled. "I think it does, too."

*Kerthump!*

A loud noise made them freeze in place.

"Did you hear that?" Claud whispered.

Mal nodded. "I thought the kids had gone outside." She shouted toward the kitchen, "Vanessa, is that you?"

No answer.

"Margo? Nicky? Claire?"

126

"They're out back with the triplets," Claudia whispered.

*Kerthump! Kerthump! Kerthump!*

"It's coming from the stairs." Mallory grabbed Claudia's arm and pulled her toward the foyer. "We better see what it is."

"No!" Claudia drew back in alarm.

*Crash!*

The sound of breaking glass was followed by a loud, "Baroo!"

"Oh, no! It's Pow," Mal gasped, racing into the foyer. "And half of our furniture."

Pow lay in a miserable heap at the bottom of the stairs. Piled up behind him was the telephone table, a chair, two pairs of tennis shoes, and a crumpled lampshade.

"Oh, Pow," Mallory murmured as she tried to untangle the leash wrapped around the table leg. "Margo tied you up and we forgot about you."

"Is he hurt?" Claudia asked.

Pow stood up the second the leash was unfastened from his leg, and yawned. Mallory giggled. "I don't think so." Her laughter was cut short as she realized that she and Claudia were going to have to clean up the mess.

"This is incredible," Mallory said, as she swept up bits of broken lamp. "We've done nothing all day but clean up after people."

"And dogs," Claudia added, as she hung

Pow's leash in the hall. "This is really a lot of work."

"And I'm going to tell my parents so," Mallory declared. She and Claud carried the rest of the furniture back upstairs. Mal had just put the phone back on the table and tucked her brother's tennis shoes in his bedroom closet, when Mr. and Mrs. Pike arrived home.

Mallory and Claud filled them in on their talk with the triplets, and how the boys had reorganized the kickball team.

"Boy!" Mr. Pike shook his head in amazement. "You girls accomplished a lot today."

As Claud was leaving she overheard Mal saying to her mom and dad, "The triplets were just a small part of our afternoon. I want to tell you about what else happened today — and how hard Claud and I had to work."

# CHAPTER 14

Jenny got a job — finally! Bostwicks, a huge clothing store near Stamford, was putting together their fall catalogue. They needed lots of children, so both Jenny and Andrea were hired. Mrs. Prezzioso asked me to go with them to the shoot, which was scheduled for Saturday. I couldn't wait.

Jenny rode in the front seat with her mom. Gone was the Miss Mess of the past week, and in her place sat a little lady.

"Are you looking forward to your first job?" I asked her, leaning forward from the backseat.

"Oh, yes." Jenny smiled. "I know it will be hard work but I can't wait to do it."

Boy, she really *was* on her best behavior. I wondered how long it would last. Could she make it through the entire shoot?

The photography studio was in a converted warehouse on the edge of town. Once again, the waiting area was filled with parents and children. But these were happy people. Happy because they'd all gotten jobs. The tension I'd felt at the two auditions was gone. In its place was a nervous excitement.

A lady wearing a smock covered in safety pins greeted us after we'd checked in with the receptionist. "Hello, you must be the Prezzioso girls."

The way she said it made them sound like an act, like the Jacksons.

"Yes, we are," Jenny answered proudly. "I'm Jennifer, and this is my sister Andrea."

"Pleased to meet you." The lady shook her hand. "You can call me Madge. Everyone does. I'm in charge of wardrobe. So if you'll come with me, I'll find something lovely for you to wear."

I couldn't get over the difference between an audition and a job. The people I'd encountered at the auditions had been brusque and cold. The people at the photo shoot were helpful and extremely considerate.

Jenny and Andrea reappeared fifteen minutes later, dressed in matching frilly sunsuits.

"Ahhhh," several people murmured from around the room. "Aren't they darling? What a lovely pair they make."

Jenny was very pleased to hear their compliments. She couldn't stop smiling. Soon a man in a turtleneck sweater appeared. He was carrying a clipboard and a folder filled with slips of paper that he called release forms.

"Your girls will be in the fun in the sand shoot," he explained to Mrs. Prezzioso. "They're setting it up now, and we should be ready to shoot in about five minutes."

"Thank you, Sam," Mrs. Prezzioso said. "We're ready."

Sam patted Jenny on the shoulder. "I've worked on several shoots with your sister and really enjoyed it. I know it'll be fun working with you."

"Thanks, Sam," Jenny said, imitating her mother.

When Sam left, Jenny turned to me and whispered excitedly, "Did you hear that? He says he's glad to work with me!"

"I'm very proud of you," I whispered back. "I know you'll be terrific."

Before we knew it, Sam was ushering us into the studio. It was incredible. One section really looked like a beach. I saw a wide stretch of sand, complete with beach umbrellas, beach chairs, and even a sand castle. The painted backdrop looked like a glistening ocean, dotted with whitecapped waves.

"Is that a real beach?" a little boy in a swimsuit asked, wide-eyed.

"No," Sam replied. "It's called a set. We

have a crew of set-dressers whose only job is to recreate a beach. They did pretty well, huh?"

The little boy nodded.

A short plump woman in black leggings and a black sweatshirt with *Picture This!* in neon pink writing across the front jogged over to meet us. "Hi, I'm Dixie. I'm the assistant director. Why don't you follow me to the beach?" Then she winked at Jenny and added, "I hope you can swim."

Mrs. Prezzioso carried Andrea to the sand and placed her on a colorful beach towel. The prop man handed Andrea a bright yellow bucket and a red plastic shovel, which she promptly stuck in her mouth. Jenny was asked to kneel next to the sandcastle and act as if she were building it. The little boy was positioned on the other side of the castle.

Ten minutes went by as the technicians moved lights and positioned the big metal reflector. At one point a man in a folding canvas chair with *Director* written across the back called, "Give the kids a little sunburn."

Jenny looked up, alarmed. I felt panicky myself. But the director just wanted more red in the lights. That took another ten minutes. When the lighting guys were finished, the kids really did look as if they'd been in the sun all afternoon. Their cheeks and shoulders had a nice rosy glow.

"That looks good," the photographer called from behind the camera. "Okay, clear the set."

The prop people moved out of range while Dixie crouched near the kids, whispering words of encouragement. "Smile big, kids!" she urged. "You like this castle. It's the best castle you ever built."

Jenny smiled and followed Dixie's and the director's instructions exactly. She scooped sand. She put a flag on top of the castle. She played with sunglasses on and with sunglasses off. Whatever they told her to do, she did. While Jenny posed with the castle, Andrea played happily with the bucket and shovel.

"You are a really good model, Jenny," Dixie said, while the prop people brought out inflatable ducks, reset the sandcastle and smoothed the sand. "You and your sister are naturals."

Jenny's face blushed an even brighter pink. Not with embarrassment, but with pleasure. "Thank you, Dixie."

By the end of the session, Jenny was starting to look tired and Andrea was getting fidgety. She kept trying to crawl off the beach set. The boy said he was thirsty and needed a break.

I was amazed that those kids had lasted so long.

When they finally announced that the shoot was over, everyone was relieved. "Can we go home now, Mommy?" Jenny asked. "I'm kind of tired."

"Of course we can go home, my angel," Mrs. Prezzioso replied. "You worked hard and did a really wonderful job today."

Madge the wardrobe lady waved to Jenny as we were leaving. "I hope I see you again. You were a delight to work with."

Jenny waved back and made a beeline for the exit. I was puzzled. The photo shoot had been a big success, and I expected that Jenny would want to linger for a while longer, to hear everyone's compliments. But she was anxious to leave. I couldn't figure her out.

Even stranger was what happened when we arrived back in Stoneybrook. Mrs. Prezzioso was slowly driving past Brenner Field when Jenny cried out, "Mommy! Stop the car!"

Mrs. Prezzioso hit the brakes. "What's the matter?"

"Look!" Jenny pointed out the window. "The triplets are having a kickball game."

"Are you sure that's the triplets' team?" I asked. I couldn't believe they'd worked everything out so quickly.

"Sure!" Jenny cried excitedly. "There's

Adam and Byron. Look, Claire is going to kick and I think Suzi is pitching!"

"Do you want to go watch?" Mrs. Prezzioso asked.

"No," Jenny replied. "I want to play!"

I winced. The last time Jenny had wanted to play, several of the kids had created a terrible scene. Of course, that was when she was Miss Priss and had made such a big deal about staying clean.

"Why don't you ask Adam if it's all right to join the game?" I suggested, getting out of the car and opening Jenny's door.

"Adam!" Jenny shouted, bolting across the grass. "Can I play?"

There was a hurried conference between Adam and his brothers. Then Adam gave her the thumbs-up sign. "Sure, if you don't say you're getting dirty."

"I won't. I promise. I just have to change my clothes," Jenny called. "And I'll be right back."

She leapt into the car, shouting, "They said I can play! Hurry, Mommy, I have to change so I can get in the game."

Jenny's enthusiasm surprised both her mother and me. We looked at each other and shrugged. "A new phase?" Mrs. Prezzioso mouthed to me.

I hoped so. As Miss Priss, Jenny had been

tense and difficult to be around. Miss Mess had been more adventuresome, but awfully hard to handle. Maybe Jenny was finding a middle area — somewhere between terminally tidy and dangerously dirty.

Mr. Prezzioso was waiting for us when we got home. "How'd the shoot go?" he asked, giving Jenny a hug.

"It went great," Jenny replied. "Now I have to change and get to the kickball game. Want to come?"

"Well . . . yes. I mean, of course!" Mr. Prezzioso was as confused and pleased by her behavior as Mrs. Prezzioso and I were.

Jenny raced upstairs and changed her clothes in record time. Moments later, as I was walking back to my house, I saw her and her dad cross the street, headed for Brenner Field. I couldn't help smiling. Jenny was wearing a T-shirt, jeans, and a baseball cap.

"Things are definitely looking up," I said to myself.

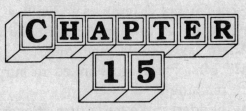

# CHAPTER 15

You know the old saying, "Good things come in small packages?" Well, sometimes good things come in strange packages, too. Mrs. Prezzioso called me Thursday afternoon, just before I was due at her house, with a favor to ask. Jenny had been turned down for a modeling job and a commercial. "Would you help me break the bad news to her?" she asked.

I agreed to help. But I wasn't looking forward to it. I wondered how Jenny would react. Would Miss Priss return? Or Miss Mess?

Neither one of them made an appearance. In fact, Jenny's reaction surprised both Mrs. Prezzioso and me.

"Hooray!" she shouted, when she heard the bad news. "Now I can play kickball."

"Honey?" Mrs. Prezzioso took her daughter by the shoulders and knelt in front of her. "Do you understand that you didn't get the job?"

"Yes," Jenny replied.

"And you realize that Andrea did get a job?"

"Uh-huh."

"And you're not sad?"

"Of course not," Jenny said with a grin. "Today's game is the girls against the boys. And Adam said I could pitch first."

"Oh?" Mrs. Prezzioso blinked in surprise. "You're pitching?"

Jenny nodded. "We get a turn at every position. That's the rule."

"Well, that's wonderful, dear," Mrs. Prezzioso said, still a little bewildered. "Just wonderful."

Jenny raced for the stairs and I turned to Mrs. Prezzioso. "I guess Jenny's decided to give up her modeling career."

"I guess so. Mr. Prezzioso and I have been encouraging her to do other things, and praising her for it. And Jenny did well on that one job. Maybe that's all that mattered to her."

Jenny appeared moments later in her jeans and a T-shirt. As she skipped happily down the stairs, Mrs. Prezzioso whispered, "Now Jenny can concentrate on important things, like being a four-year-old."

"And kicking a home run," I whispered back.

On Friday, I couldn't wait to break the news about Jenny to the BSC. I arrived at Claudia's house early and had trouble waiting for the meeting to start.

At five-thirty, Kristy flopped into the director's chair and tugged on her visor. "This meeting of the BSC is officially called to order. Any news or announcements?"

I started to speak, but suddenly someone appeared in the doorway. There, with glistening eyes and a grin that spread from ear to ear, stood Mallory.

"Hi, everybody!" she cried. "I'm back!"

Everybody jumped up and rushed forward to hug Mallory. I cried (of course), but so did a couple of others. When we finally calmed down, Kristy cleared her throat. "I would like to take this moment to officially welcome Mallory back to the Baby-sitters Club."

We cheered and applauded

"How did you talk your parents into it?" Jessi asked.

"Well," Mallory clasped her hands in front of her, "I took Kristy's advice. I didn't talk to my parents about being sick or well, although that did come up in the discussion. I showed them my schedule and they were flabbergasted to find out how much time I'd spent baby-sitting."

"Is that when they said yes?" Claud asked.

"No, first they had to call Dr. Dellenkamp, just to be on the safe side. She told Mom and

Dad that my blood tests have been normal for weeks, and she didn't see any reason why I couldn't go back to my regular schedule. So here I am!"

More applause. Then Kristy took the floor again. This time she was holding the BSC notebook. "I think this is such an important moment in Baby-sitters Club history that we should record it. I'm going to send the notebook around the room and I want you each to write something in it."

Kristy sat down with the notebook first and at the top of the page she scrawled:

*This is a very big day for the Baby-sitters Club. Mallory has rejoined us. Welcome back, Mallory, we really missed you!*

*Love, Kristy*

Solemnly we passed the journal around the circle. Each of us wrote a special note to Mallory. When the book reached me, I wrote:

*The BSC just wasn't the same without you. Welcome back to a terrific baby-sitter and a great friend!*

*Love, Mary Anne*

By the time the book had made the full circle, we were all looking a little misty-eyed again.

"This calls for a celebration," Claudia said, climbing down from her bed and crawling underneath it. "I think I have a whole bag of Mallomars somewhere under here. I hid them a week ago."

"It took her two months to find those potato chips," Shannon joked. "It'll probably be at least three more weeks before she tracks down the Mallomars."

Kristy (Miss Great Ideas) said, "I've got an idea. Why don't we go out this weekend and really celebrate? We could split a pizza!"

"The treasury is in good shape right now," Stacey said, checking the dues envelope. "We could even throw in sodas."

"All right!" Kristy gave Stacey a high-five.

I listened as we planned our Welcome Back Celebration for Mal and sighed happily. Jenny's problem was solved. The kickball team was off and running. And best of all, Mal was a member of the BSC again. Things were almost perfect. Now, if Dawn would just come home . . .

## About the Author

ANN M. MARTIN did *a lot* of baby-sitting when she was growing up in Princeton, New Jersey. She is a former editor of books for children, and was graduated from Smith College.

Ms. Martin lives in New York City with her cats, Mouse and Rosie. She likes ice cream and *I Love Lucy*; and she hates to cook.

Ann Martin's Apple Paperbacks include *Yours Turly, Shirley; Ten Kids, No Pets; With You and Without You; Bummer Summer*; and all the other books in the Baby-sitters Club series.

Look for #74

KRISTY AND THE COPYCAT

I looked at Bea's note, then I looked at Tonya and at Dilys.

Dilys nodded, then slowly, sheepishly, pulled out three similar notes of her own. And Tonya unfolded a tiny square that she dug up from the corner of her pocket — another note!

"We've all gotten them then: threats, demands for money," I said.

"Yeah, well, I don't have that kind of money," said Tonya quickly.

"Neither do I," cried Bea.

"Me, either," said Dilys.

"What do you want to do?" said Tonya. "It's not like he, or she, left any instructions on how we're supposed to *pay* this money.

"That's true," I said thoughtfully. "Hmmm. Maybe we should just wait. Whoever is doing it will have to write at least one more note to say how we're supposed to pay this money.

If we're observant, and lucky, we might catch him."

Bea said, "I hate this."

"Right, Bea. Like we all love it," said Tonya. "Kristy's right. We'll wait. It's all we can do."

Dilys sighed, then nodded. "Yeah."

"Okay, then," I said.

The door to the girls locker room slammed. We looked up. Tallie and Marcia were standing there. They stared at us and we stared back at them for a long moment.

I cleared my throat. "See you later," I said loudly to Bea and Tonya and Dilys.

As I moved away, I raised my hand and waved at Tallie and Marcia. Tallie gave me a little half-wave back. But Marcia just frowned suspiciously.

I gave up. I turned and walked toward home, faster and faster as if I could leave my thoughts and all the terrible things that had happened behind. But of course, I couldn't. Because no matter who had seen what had happened, no matter *who* was blackmailing me, the worst part was that I had brought it on myself. I'd let myself be talked into something I didn't believe in. I'd copied others to try and fit in instead of being myself.

And now, I didn't like myself very much anymore at all.

**Read all the latest books
in the Baby-sitters Club series
by Ann M. Martin**

#44 *Dawn and the Big Sleepover*
One hundred kids, thirty pizzas — it's Dawn's biggest baby-sitting job ever!

#45 *Kristy and the Baby Parade*
Will the Baby-sitters' float take first prize in the Stoneybrook Baby Parade?

#46 *Mary Anne Misses Logan*
But does Logan miss *her*?

#47 *Mallory on Strike*
Mallory needs a break from baby-sitting — even if it means quitting the club.

#48 *Jessi's Wish*
Jessi makes a very special wish for a little girl with cancer.

#49 *Claudia and the Genius of Elm Street*
Baby-sitting for a seven-year-old genius makes Claudia feel like a world-class dunce.

#50 *Dawn's Big Date*
Will Dawn's date with Logan's cousin be a total disaster?

#51 *Stacey's Ex-Best Friend*
Is Stacey's old friend Laine super mature or just a super snob?

#52 *Mary Anne + 2 Many Babies*
Whoever thought taking care of a bunch of babies could be so much trouble?

#53  *Kristy For President*
Can Kristy run the BSC and the whole eighth grade?

#54  *Mallory and the Dream Horse*
Mallory is taking professional riding lessons. It's a dream come true!

#55  *Jessi's Gold Medal*
Jessi's going for the gold in a synchronized swimming competition!

#56  *Keep Out, Claudia!*
Who wouldn't want Claudia for a baby-sitter?

#57  *Dawn Saves the Planet*
Dawn's trying to do a good thing — but she's driving everyone crazy!

#58  *Stacey's Choice*
Stacey's parents are both depending on her. But how can she choose between them . . . again?

#59  *Mallory Hates Boys (and Gym)*
Boys and gym. What a disgusting combination!

#60  *Mary Anne's Makeover*
Everyone loves the new Mary Anne — *except* the BSC!

#61  *Jessi and the Awful Secret*
Only Jessi knows what's really wrong with one of the girls in her dance class.

#62  *Kristy and the Worst Kid Ever*
Need a baby-sitter for Lou? Don't call the Baby-sitters Club!

#63  *Claudia's F̶r̶i̶e̶n̶d̶ Friend*
Claudia and Shea can't spell — but they can be friends!

#64 *Dawn's Family Feud*
Family squabbles are one thing. But the Schafers and the Spiers are practically waging war!

#65 *Stacey's Big Crush*
Stacey's in LUV . . . with her twenty-two-year-old teacher!

#66 *Maid Mary Anne*
Mary Anne's a baby-sitter — not a housekeeper!

#67 *Dawn's Big Move*
Dawn's moving back to California. But she'll be back, right?

#68 *Jessi and the Bad Baby-sitter*
This is Dawn's replacement?

#69 *Get Well Soon, Mallory!*
How will the BSC survive without Mallory?

#70 *Stacey and the Cheerleaders*
Stacey becomes part of the "in" crowd when she tries out for the cheerleading team.

#71 *Claudia and the Perfect Boy*
Love is in the air when Claudia starts a personals column in the school paper.

#72 *Dawn and the We ♥ Kids Club*
Is Dawn's California baby-sitting club more popular than Stoneybrook's BSC?

#73 *Mary Anne and Miss Priss*
What will Mary Anne do with a kid who is *too* perfect?

#74 *Kristy and the Copycat*
Kristy's done something bad — something she'd never want Karen to copy.

Super Specials:

# 8 *Baby-sitters at Shadow Lake*
Campfires, cute guys, and a mystery — the Baby-sitters are in for a week of summer fun!

# 9 *Starring the Baby-sitters Club!*
The Baby-sitters get involved onstage and off in the SMS school production of *Peter Pan*.

#10 *Sea City, Here We Come!*
The Baby-sitters head back to the Jersey shore for some fun in the sun!

Mysteries:

# 9 *Kristy and the Haunted Mansion*
Kristy and the Krashers are spending the night in a spooky old house!

#10 *Stacey and the Mystery Money*
Who would give Stacey counterfeit money?

#11 *Claudia and the Mystery at the Museum*
Burglaries, forgeries . . . something crooked is going on at the new museum in Stoneybrook!

#12 *Dawn and the Surfer Ghost*
When a local surfer mysteriously disappears, Dawn fears his ghost is haunting the beach.

#13 *Mary Anne and the Library Mystery*
There's a Readathon going on and someone's setting fires in the Stoneybrook library!

#14 *Stacey and the Mystery at the Mall*
Shoplifting, burglaries — mysterious things are going on at the Washington Mall!

Special Edition (Readers' Request):
*Logan Bruno, Boy Baby-sitter*
Has Logan decided he's too cool for baby-sitting?

# THE BABY-SITTERS CLUB®

## by Ann M. Martin

| | | | |
|---|---|---|---|
| ❏ MG43388-1 | #1 | Kristy's Great Idea | $3.50 |
| ❏ MG43387-3 | #10 | Logan Likes Mary Anne! | $3.50 |
| ❏ MG43717-8 | #15 | Little Miss Stoneybrook...and Dawn | $3.50 |
| ❏ MG43722-4 | #20 | Kristy and the Walking Disaster | $3.50 |
| ❏ MG43347-4 | #25 | Mary Anne and the Search for Tigger | $3.50 |
| ❏ MG42498-X | #30 | Mary Anne and the Great Romance | $3.50 |
| ❏ MG42497-1 | #31 | Dawn's Wicked Stepsister | $3.50 |
| ❏ MG42496-3 | #32 | Kristy and the Secret of Susan | $3.50 |
| ❏ MG42495-5 | #33 | Claudia and the Great Search | $3.25 |
| ❏ MG42494-7 | #34 | Mary Anne and Too Many Boys | $3.50 |
| ❏ MG42508-0 | #35 | Stacey and the Mystery of Stoneybrook | $3.50 |
| ❏ MG43565-5 | #36 | Jessi's Baby-sitter | $3.50 |
| ❏ MG43566-3 | #37 | Dawn and the Older Boy | $3.25 |
| ❏ MG43567-1 | #38 | Kristy's Mystery Admirer | $3.25 |
| ❏ MG43568-X | #39 | Poor Mallory! | $3.25 |
| ❏ MG44082-9 | #40 | Claudia and the Middle School Mystery | $3.25 |
| ❏ MG43570-1 | #41 | Mary Anne Versus Logan | $3.50 |
| ❏ MG44083-7 | #42 | Jessi and the Dance School Phantom | $3.50 |
| ❏ MG43572-8 | #43 | Stacey's Emergency | $3.50 |
| ❏ MG43573-6 | #44 | Dawn and the Big Sleepover | $3.50 |
| ❏ MG43574-4 | #45 | Kristy and the Baby Parade | $3.50 |
| ❏ MG43569-8 | #46 | Mary Anne Misses Logan | $3.50 |
| ❏ MG44971-0 | #47 | Mallory on Strike | $3.50 |
| ❏ MG43571-X | #48 | Jessi's Wish | $3.50 |
| ❏ MG44970-2 | #49 | Claudia and the Genius of Elm Street | $3.25 |
| ❏ MG44969-9 | #50 | Dawn's Big Date | $3.50 |
| ❏ MG44968-0 | #51 | Stacey's Ex-Best Friend | $3.50 |
| ❏ MG44966-4 | #52 | Mary Anne + 2 Many Babies | $3.50 |
| ❏ MG44967-2 | #53 | Kristy for President | $3.25 |
| ❏ MG44965-6 | #54 | Mallory and the Dream Horse | $3.25 |
| ❏ MG44964-8 | #55 | Jessi's Gold Medal | $3.25 |
| ❏ MG45657-1 | #56 | Keep Out, Claudia! | $3.50 |
| ❏ MG45658-X | #57 | Dawn Saves the Planet | $3.50 |

*More titles...* ➤

*The Baby-sitters Club titles continued...*

| | | |
|---|---|---|
| ☐ MG45659-8 | #58 Stacey's Choice | $3.50 |
| ☐ MG45660-1 | #59 Mallory Hates Boys (and Gym) | $3.50 |
| ☐ MG45662-8 | #60 Mary Anne's Makeover | $3.50 |
| ☐ MG45663-6 | #61 Jessi's and the Awful Secret | $3.50 |
| ☐ MG45664-4 | #62 Kristy and the Worst Kid Ever | $3.50 |
| ☐ MG45665-2 | #63 Claudia's Freind Friend | $3.50 |
| ☐ MG45666-0 | #64 Dawn's Family Feud | $3.50 |
| ☐ MG45667-9 | #65 Stacey's Big Crush | $3.50 |
| ☐ MG47004-3 | #66 Maid Mary Anne | $3.50 |
| ☐ MG47005-1 | #67 Dawn's Big Move | $3.50 |
| ☐ MG47006-X | #68 Jessi and the Bad Baby-Sitter | $3.50 |
| ☐ MG47007-8 | #69 Get Well Soon, Mallory! | $3.50 |
| ☐ MG47008-6 | #70 Stacey and the Cheerleaders | $3.50 |
| ☐ MG47009-4 | #71 Claudia and the Perfect Boy | $3.50 |
| ☐ MG47010-8 | #72 Dawn and the We Love Kids Club | $3.50 |
| ☐ MG45575-3 | Logan's Story  Special Edition Readers' Request | $3.25 |
| ☐ MG47118-X | Logan Bruno, Boy Baby-sitter  Special Edition Readers' Request | $3.50 |
| ☐ MG44240-6 | Baby-sitters on Board!  Super Special #1 | $3.95 |
| ☐ MG44239-2 | Baby-sitters' Summer Vacation  Super Special #2 | $3.95 |
| ☐ MG43973-1 | Baby-sitters' Winter Vacation  Super Special #3 | $3.95 |
| ☐ MG42493-9 | Baby-sitters' Island Adventure  Super Special #4 | $3.95 |
| ☐ MG43575-2 | California Girls!  Super Special #5 | $3.95 |
| ☐ MG43576-0 | New York, New York!  Super Special #6 | $3.95 |
| ☐ MG44963-X | Snowbound  Super Special #7 | $3.95 |
| ☐ MG44962-X | Baby-sitters at Shadow Lake  Super Special  #8 | $3.95 |
| ☐ MG45661-X | Starring the Baby-sitters Club  Super Special  #9 | $3.95 |
| ☐ MG45674-1 | Sea City, Here We Come!  Super Special  #10 | $3.95 |

Available wherever you buy books...or use this order form.

Scholastic Inc., P.O. Box 7502, 2931 E. McCarty Street, Jefferson City, MO 65102

Please send me the books I have checked above. I am enclosing $_____ (please add $2.00 to cover shipping and handling). Send check or money order - no cash or C.O.D.s please.

Name _____ Birthdate_____

Address _____

City_____ State/Zip _____

Please allow four to six weeks for delivery. Offer good in the U.S. only. Sorry, mail orders are not available to residents of Canada. Prices subject to change.

BSC993

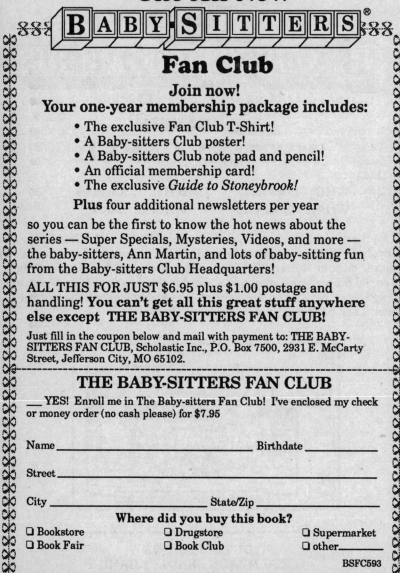

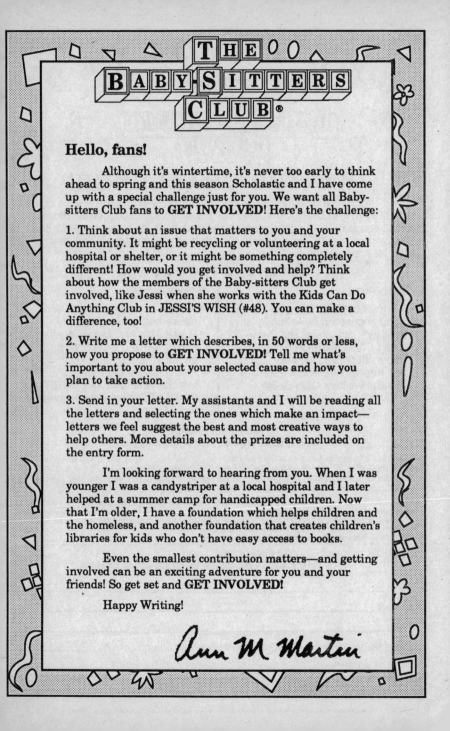

# THE BABY-SITTERS Club®

## Hello, fans!

Although it's wintertime, it's never too early to think ahead to spring and this season Scholastic and I have come up with a special challenge just for you. We want all Baby-sitters Club fans to **GET INVOLVED!** Here's the challenge:

1. Think about an issue that matters to you and your community. It might be recycling or volunteering at a local hospital or shelter, or it might be something completely different! How would you get involved and help? Think about how the members of the Baby-sitters Club get involved, like Jessi when she works with the Kids Can Do Anything Club in JESSI'S WISH (#48). You can make a difference, too!

2. Write me a letter which describes, in 50 words or less, how you propose to **GET INVOLVED!** Tell me what's important to you about your selected cause and how you plan to take action.

3. Send in your letter. My assistants and I will be reading all the letters and selecting the ones which make an impact— letters we feel suggest the best and most creative ways to help others. More details about the prizes are included on the entry form.

I'm looking forward to hearing from you. When I was younger I was a candystriper at a local hospital and I later helped at a summer camp for handicapped children. Now that I'm older, I have a foundation which helps children and the homeless, and another foundation that creates children's libraries for kids who don't have easy access to books.

Even the smallest contribution matters—and getting involved can be an exciting adventure for you and your friends! So get set and **GET INVOLVED!**

Happy Writing!

*Ann M. Martin*

# GET INVOLVED!

## IT'S THE BABY-SITTERS Club®

# WINTER CHALLENGE!

If you're a BSC fan, you know that the Baby-sitters are always active and busy in their community...and not just with baby-sitting. When Stoneybrook needs help, the girls are ready to pitch in. If you're concerned about the town you live in, write a one-page letter about 50 words telling us your plan for improving it.

## ENTER AND YOU CAN WIN:

### GRAND PRIZE

- A $10,000 US Scholarship Savings Bond sponsored by Milton Bradley®, makers of The Baby-sitters Club Board Game and The Baby-sitters Club Mystery Game, and Kenner Products, makers of The Baby-sitters Club Dolls.

### 2 FIRST PRIZES

- A book dedicated to you, your cause and your community.
- A visit from Ann Martin to your hometown and local bookstore for an autographing and lunch.
- Plus..loads of quality BSC merchandise and a **BSC GET INVOLVED** sweatshirt, signed by Ann Martin.

## 100 RUNNERS-UP:
### Win a **BSC GET INVOLVED** sweatshirt.

Just fill in the coupon below or write the information on a 3" x 5" piece of paper and mail with your **"GET INVOLVED"** letter to the appropriate address. U.S. Residents send entries to: **SCHOLASTIC INC.**, **BSC WINTER CHALLENGE**, P.O. Box 742, Cooper Station, NY 10276. Canadian residents send entries to Iris Ferguson, Scholastic Inc., 123 Newkirk Road, Richmond Hill, Ontario, Canada LAC 3G5.

**Rules:** Entries must be postmarked by March 31, 1994. Winners will be judged by Scholastic Inc., and Ann M. Martin and notified by mail. No purchase necessary. Valid in the U.S. and Canada. Void where prohibited. Employees of Scholastic Inc., its agencies, affiliates, subsidiaries, and their immediate families are not eligible. For a complete list of winners, send a self-addressed stamped envelope after March 31, 1994. to: THE BSC WINTER CHALLENGE Winners List, at either address provided above.

Attach this coupon to your **GET INVOLVED!** Letter.

## THE BABY-SITTERS CLUB WINTER CHALLENGE

Name _____  Birthdate _____

Address _____  Phone# _____

City _____  State/Zip _____

**Where did you buy this book?**  ☐ Bookstore  ☐ Other (Specify) _____

**Name of Bookstore** _____

**HAVE YOU JOINED THE BSC FAN CLUB YET!** See back of this book for details.

BSC993